"Do you know what you're doing?" Rose asked with a giggle.

"Don't you worry about me, Rosie," Mark shot back from the kitchen.

"He'll make someone a good *frau* one day." Jacob's laughter boomed. Rose smiled even though she didn't find it very funny. Mark ignored him as he got the cups ready for the coffee.

Jacob turned back to Rose. "So, is it Rose, or Rosie?"

"It's Rose, but Mark likes to call me Rosie for some reason."

"I'll call you Rose. I like the name Rose."

"Okay." It didn't matter what he called her. She liked the deep rich tones of his voice.

"What are you doing Sunday afternoon?" Jacob asked.

"Nothing that I know of."

Jacob leaned closer and said quietly, "How about we do something together?"

The coffee container slipped suddenly from Mark's grasp in the kitchen and clanged heavily on the floor, scattering coffee everywhere.

Rose jumped up to help Mark, while Jacob laughed. It was like being stuck between two roosters that wanted to fight each other.

Could the night get any more awkward?

Samantha Price is a bestselling author who knew she wanted to become a writer at the age of seven, while her grandmother read her Peter Rabbit. Though the adventures of Peter started Samantha on her creative journey, it is now her love of Amish culture that inspires her. Her writing is wholesome with more than a dash of sweetness. Samantha lives in a quaint Victorian cottage with three rambunctious dogs.

AMISH ROSE

Samantha Price

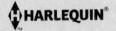

Recycling programs
for this product may
not exist in your area.

ISBN-13: 978-1-335-45574-1

Amish Rose

Printed in U.S.A.

Chapter One

Surely goodness and mercy shall follow me all the days of my life: and I will dwell in the house of the Lord for ever.

Psalm 23:6

"He seems happy." A deep voice boomed from behind Rose, jolting her from her daydreams.

Rose turned around to see her good friend, Mark. "Who does?"

"Your *bruder.*" Mark nodded his head while making a forward movement with the glass in his hand, both motions toward the wedding table where Trevor sat with his new wife.

It hadn't been easy for Trevor to decide on a wife. He'd had many women to choose from. Had it not been for the pressure on him from their parents, Rose was sure that Trevor would've happily stayed unmarried into his thirties. He'd made a good choice in Amy, Rose thought.

Even though Amy, her new sister-in-law, was a few years older than she, Amy had always been kind to Rose when she'd experienced trouble during her school years. It hadn't been easy for Rose being the eldest of four girls with two older brothers. Since her father was a deacon, there had always been pressure on her to be perfect. Rose had feared that she wouldn't live up to the standards that her older brothers had set.

"I guess he is," Rose commented looking back to see Trevor laughing with Amy.

"It might be you soon."

Rose whipped her head around to look again at Mark. "What, marrying?"

"*Jah*, wedded bliss, some call it."

Rose glanced at the newly married pair, frowned, and then turned back to tell Mark exactly what she thought of that idea. "It'll be a long time before that happens." She shook her head to reinforce her feelings. Mark was handsome but not someone she would marry. He was slightly taller than she, but she'd always seen herself with a man who was much taller. Reaching five feet ten inches herself, there weren't that many men around who were taller.

"Don't you want to be happy, Rosie?" Mark was the only one who called her Rosie rather than Rose.

"I'm happy right now. Do you think a woman needs a man to make her happy?"

"*Jah*, I do."

Rose laughed, only because she knew Mark was teasing her. "Mark Schumacher, if I didn't know you any better I'd walk away right now."

"You'll marry me one day, Rosie Yoder. You just wait and see."

Rose shook her head at him. "Don't hold your breath waiting."

He laughed. Mark teasing Rose about marrying him had become an ongoing joke between them ever since Mark had taken the stall right by the one she handled at the farmers market. Rose took his teasing in good humor. Whenever they weren't busy with customers, they'd talk and laugh to pass the time.

"Rose, there you are. *Mamm's* looking for you. She said you promised to help with the food." Tulip, Rose's younger sister by one year, looked shaken up and there was good reason. Their mother was helping organize the wedding feast for the three hundred guests. And to their mother, 'helping' meant taking over the task and delegating to the other ladies.

"Right now?" Rose asked.

"*Jah*, of course, right now. The food is being dished into the serving bowls as we speak and she's asked for you. Come on!" Tulip frowned and her dark eyes fixed upon Rose as though pleading.

"Okay. There's no need for dramatics."

Tulip took hold of Rose's arm and led her away.

"Hello, Tulip," Mark said as Tulip dragged Rose away.

"Hello, Mark," Tulip called over her shoulder.

When Mark was out of earshot, Rose said, "That was rude, Tulip. Mark and I were talking."

"You see him every day. What could you possibly have left to talk about?"

"I dunno—stuff."

"If I were you, I wouldn't tell *Mamm* you were off gossiping somewhere. She's mighty cranky that you weren't there to help from the start. *Mamm* said as her oldest *dochder* you should've stayed right by her side to learn from her."

Rose nodded as she hurried toward the annex outside Amy's parents' kitchen where the food was being prepared. The kitchen in the house was far too small to suffice for the preparation of food for the large number of people who turned out for the Amish wedding.

"Here she is now," the bride's mother said to Tulip and Rose's mother.

"About time, too!" Nancy Yoder glared at her eldest daughter.

"Sorry, *Mamm.* I helped with the food earlier. I didn't know you needed me to do it for the whole time."

"If a job's worth doing it's—"

"I know. It's worth doing well. I know." Rose nodded, hoping to stop a lecture before it began.

"You stay until the job's complete!" Nancy shook her head at her and Rose knew if there hadn't been so many women fussing about, her mother would've delivered a lengthy stern lecture. "You're here now; that's the important thing."

"Please take the plates out to the tables, Rose," Amy's mother asked.

"Okay."

"You'll have to help her, Tulip," Nancy added.

Together, Rose and Tulip scooped up armfuls of white dinner plates and headed toward the tables spread across the yard. The wedding had taken place in the bride's home, as was the tradition in their community. Weddings were publicised and spread by word of mouth and there was never any way to tell exactly how many guests would attend. Typically, it was in the hundreds.

When Rose put the plates down on the table, she glanced over to see her two younger sisters, twins, giggling and running around with other girls in the distance. The twins were sixteen, but they still associated with people much younger than themselves. Rose knew that if her mother had been aware of how the twins were behaving, they too would've got a stern reprimand. They would've been told that they weren't behaving like young ladies, and since their father was a deacon and part of the oversight, their family had to set an example to others.

The twins, Daisy and Lily, had dark coloring and were pretty. They weren't as tall as Rose, but neither was Tulip. Rose wasn't jealous of her sisters, but had often wished she had their dark coloring rather than her red hair and the pale skin that always accompanied her shade of hair.

When she heard one of the twins let out an ear-splitting squeal, her mind drifted back to the lecture she thought the twins might get. It was a lecture that Rose had heard many a time before. She often wished her father hadn't been selected as part of the church oversight—their lives might be more enjoyable without the constant pressure. Rose always felt as though she were being watched—judged.

She glanced over at her second-eldest brother. Life had been a whole lot easier for her brothers; she was certain of that. Rose considered that life, in general, was easier for men—that was her secret thought. Amish women were restricted in what they could and couldn't do, more so than the men. Rose kept her rebellious thoughts to herself, apart from her many serious conversations with Mary, her best friend who'd gone on a *rumspringa*.

A *rumspringa* wasn't an option for Rose. Not because she wasn't allowed, it was just that she didn't want to live in the *Englisch* world. Her next best friend was Mark, although there were many things that she never discussed with him because—being a man—he wouldn't understand. Mark was always good for someone to laugh with.

Rose turned around and went back for more plates. Each of the girls could only carry about twelve at a time, and there were a great many more plates that needed to be placed on each of the tables.

"We need some people to help us, *Mamm*," Rose said to her mother as she heaped some more plates into her arms.

Nancy ordered a few more women to help them with the plates. Nancy had taken over the organization of the food preparation from Amy's mother. That was Nancy's way—taking over and being in charge was what she did best.

Within minutes, all the cutlery and plates were on the tables, and now the only thing remaining was for the food to be brought out.

The bishop clapped his hands, causing the hum of the crowd's conversation to cease. He said a few words and everyone bowed their heads. When the bishop finished his prayer, he gave Nancy a nod letting her know she could send the ladies out with the food.

When Rose had placed the last of the food onto one of the tables, she glanced at her mother to see her leaning against the house with her arms folded. A hint of a private smile turned the corners of her mother's lips upward.

Today, her mother was pleased to be getting her second son married off. A year before, the oldest, Peter, had gotten married. Peter and his wife were now expecting their first child. Somehow Nancy had persuaded her quilting bee, who met regularly every Tuesday afternoon, to start knitting baby clothing. It seemed no one was game to say 'no' to Nancy.

"Are you eating, Rosie?"

"*Jah*, I've worked up an appetite."

"Sit with me?" Mark asked as he handed Rose a plate.

Rose nodded and followed Mark to a table at the far

edge of the yard. There were around fifty tables that could each comfortably seat fifteen people, and each table had its own bowls of food in the center. Often there were so many guests that there were three sittings for the one meal. At some weddings, there were long food tables and people served themselves buffet-style before they sat down at the tables. The wedding had started just before midday, so it was a perfect time to eat a large meal.

She and Mark each heaped food onto their plates.

"It's a nice wedding," Mark said before he took a large mouthful.

"Aren't they all the same?" Rose asked.

Mark smiled and finished chewing. "You never agree with anything I say."

"I do when you're right."

"Aren't I always?"

Rose giggled. "*Nee*, but you're welcome to your delusions."

He shook his head and took another mouthful. Mark then talked to some of their tablemates who were visiting from another community.

Rose liked the way Mark could talk to anyone. She was too nervous to speak to someone new unless they spoke to her first.

The twins sat down at the table with them.

"It'll be you two next," Daisy said to Mark and Rose.

Mark laughed, raised his eyebrows and looked at Rose as though waiting for her to say something.

"Don't be silly. That's what people always say at weddings. They look around for who'll be next." Rose looked at the other people at the table who were now staring at her. "She's only joking," she told them. It was an awkward moment and Rose looked down at her plate and pushed the food around with her fork.

Mark laughed. "I'm always asking her, but she always says 'no.' One day she'll weaken."

The twins roared with laughter while digging each other in the ribs.

"You should marry him," Daisy, the older twin said to Rose when she'd finished laughing.

"Hush, Daisy!" Rose just wanted the nonsense conversation to end.

"Stop hushing me all the time."

"Yeah, Rose, let her speak," Lily added.

Rose stood up and stepped over the bench seat. "Excuse me. I have to help *Mamm* with something." As she walked away, she could hear her twin sisters' faint giggles.

Mark would've been her perfect man if he were just a little different—a little taller and a little more matureminded. She didn't need her sisters encouraging him. It would only lead to his disappointment.

Rose found her mother in the food annex. "Need some help?"

"Yeah! I'll need help washing the dishes as they come in."

"I'll do it."

"*Denke*, Rose. I was going to ask, but weddings are a good opportunity for you to meet people. Don't you want to mingle and see what new people you can meet? Amy has quite a few relations here you wouldn't have met."

Rose knew her mother meant it was a good place to meet potential husbands. Her mother was correct. Weddings were one of the best ways of meeting potential spouses. "I've already met quite a few people." Rose leaned in and whispered, "There are no men my age."

Her mother nodded. "Well, you might as well help me, then."

For the remainder of the celebrations, Rose stayed in the annex washing dishes. When the dishes were all nearly done, Rose took her hands out of the hot sudsy water. They were all wrinkled and her nails were pale and unsightly.

"Rose has got dishpan hands," she heard Daisy say to Lily.

"They'll come right soon, Rose. Do you want me to take over for a while?" Lily, the kinder of the twins, asked.

"Would you?"

"*Jah.* Move over." Lily rolled up her sleeves.

"I'll dry them," Daisy said.

Nancy walked up behind the three of them. "*Denke,* girls. You can go now, Rose. You've been enough help. You might be able to go home with your *vadder.* The girls and I will have someone take us home later."

"Okay. Are you sure?"

"*Jah,* now go."

By now, most of the guests had left. Rose looked around for Tulip and then caught sight of her father and Tulip heading for the buggy. She ran to catch them.

"Wait up."

They both turned and stopped until she caught up.

"*Mamm* and the twins are staying on. *Mamm* said I'd done enough work."

"I know, that's your *mudder.* She always stays late, until the end, at weddings. Let's go home," their father said.

"How did you get out of doing any work, Tulip?"

"I kept out of the way. You volunteered, I heard."

Hezekiah Yoder smiled as he listened quietly to his daughters. He never had much to say, but when he did, everyone listened.

"*Jah*, I did." Rose held out her hands.

"They look dreadful."

"They're very clean now, at least."

"We can put some olive oil on them when we get home."

Rose looked around to see if Mark had already left. She couldn't see his buggy and his chestnut horse anywhere.

Home was at least a thirty-minute buggy ride away. Rose let Tulip sit in the front while she settled in the back and looked out. She smiled as a rabbit scampered across their buggy's path and disappeared into the tall grass by the roadside. She closed her eyes and enjoyed the even rhythm of the horse's hooves as they *clip-clopped* their way up the dirt-packed road.

After a short rest, she moved closer to the opening so she could watch the cows grazing in the sun-drenched fields. Further up the road, two farmers mending fences straightened up and waved as they passed by. Their happy faces made her feel good and she waved back.

She looked across the patchwork of varying shades of green pastures and distant rolling hills, and wondered how her best friend could leave the serenity and beauty of this place to live in the city of New York.

Chapter Two

Let all those that seek thee rejoice and be glad in
thee: let such as love thy salvation say continually,
The Lord be magnified.

Psalm 40:16

"Rose, can you collect the eggs for me? I just want to
sleep in," Tulip asked the next morning from her bedroom as Rose passed by the doorway.

Rose stopped and stuck her head into Tulip's bedroom. "Okay, I'll do it this time, and then you'll owe
me one."

"Deal!" Tulip replied.

Rose had learned early to negotiate with her sisters—
to trade a favor for a favor. Otherwise, she'd be the only
one doing anything. If she collected the eggs this morning, then Tulip would do something for her another time.

"Where are you going?" Her mother stared at Rose as
she grabbed the wicker basket by the back door. "That's
Tulip's job."

"I said I do it for her today."

"Okay. I suppose that's alright, but when you come

back, I have something to tell you before the other girls
come downstairs."

"What is it?"

"It can wait until you get the eggs."

"Have I done something wrong?"

Her mother laughed, her green eyes crinkling at the
corners. Even though her mother was in her mid forties,
she was still quite an attractive woman. Rose hoped she
might look as good when she reached that age.

"Of course, you haven't done anything wrong, Rose.
I couldn't have asked for a better *dochder.*"

Rose was relieved, but hated not knowing things. She
couldn't wait to hear what her mother was going to tell
her. "Can you tell me now, *Mamm*? I can't wait."

Her mother sighed. "Okay, sit down."

Once Rose was seated at the long wooden kitchen
table, her mother sat opposite.

"Now that both of your brothers are married, I can
turn my attention to helping you, and Tulip, and then
the twins to find husbands."

"Is that it?"

"*Jah*, it wasn't a big secret I had to tell you."

Rose huffed. "I thought it was. Anyway, I don't need
help, thanks all the same. I'd rather not look for a man.
He can find *me.*"

Her mother shook her head. "That's not how it happens. You must listen to me, Rose. If you wait, you'll
end up with no one!"

Rose frowned at the urgency and panic in her mother's voice.

Her mother grabbed her by the shoulders and looked
into her eyes. "Men are in limited supply in the community. Girls Tulip's age are getting married, and girls
the twins' age are dating. I don't want you to miss out."

Rose thought about that for a moment. It would certainly feel weird for her younger sisters to get married before she did—weirder still for either of the twins to date a man. They seemed far too young and definitely acted younger than their years. "I don't even know anybody that I want to marry."

"That's because you haven't been focused on looking for someone." Her mother slapped a hand hard on the table, which made Rose jump.

"You scared me."

"But that ends today!"

"What does?"

"You not looking for someone. You're old enough to be married and there's nothing wrong with giving me some *grosskinner*. Your *bruder's boppli* will be born soon and it would be *gut* if my *grosskinner* were all close in age."

"That doesn't sound like a good reason to get married to me."

Her mother laughed. "Everyone should be married. That's what *Gott* has planned. He planned for every *mann* to have a *fraa* and every woman to have a *mann*. That's the way *Gott* made us."

"I don't know."

"What don't you know, my dear girl?"

"I don't know about this whole thing. I've never even gone on a buggy ride with a boy…err, I mean, a man."

"*Jah*, I know. That's the problem, Rose. Can't you see that?"

Her mother cast her gaze downward and Rose felt bad for being such a disappointment.

"You see, Rose, if we don't plan in life we get nowhere."

Her mother wasn't making sense. "You want me to *plan* to fall in love with someone?"

Nancy pressed her lips together and fine lines appeared around her mouth. "You're trying to make light of this, Rose."

"I'm not, *Mamm*, really, I'm not! I just don't see how you can plan to fall in love with someone."

Her mother leaned forward. "Love grows when you're married. You choose a husband with this." She tapped a finger on her head. "Not with your heart. Love grows from respect."

That was news to Rose—that her mother felt that way. A thought occurred to Rose. "Is that how you chose *Dat*?"

"*Jah.* Your *vadder* was a *gut* man of *Gott* and a hard worker. He wasn't a deacon back then though, that came when you were a *boppli*. He's never disappointed me and he's been a steady provider. Together, we've been happy."

Rose nibbled on a fingernail. She had never heard such a thing. She always thought that love was something whimsical and magical—something to be experienced once in a lifetime, when two like souls met and knew at once that they were meant for one another. "Are you saying you were never in love with *Dat* before you married him?" It was bold of Rose to ask that question at the risk of angering her mother, but she had to know. "I mean, when you first met him? I know you're in love with him now."

"*Nee*, I wasn't in love with him when I first met him. I had to get to know him. Now run and get those eggs so I can make the breakfast."

"Okay." Rose had a lot to think about. She stood up and grabbed the egg basket.

"I'm giving you a year, Rose."

Rose was nearly out the door. She stopped and turned slightly to look at her mother. "A year for what?"

"To get married."

Rose's jaw dropped open. "What if I haven't found somebody in a year?"

"You will. Start talking to some men and that'll be a beginning. If you never talk to a man how would you know which one suits you?"

Rose nodded. There was no point telling her mother that she did talk to men. If she told her mother that, she'd want to know which ones. It was easier just to keep quiet. With the basket looped over her arm, Rose hurried across the wet grass, fresh from the morning dew, as the crisp morning air bit into her cheeks.

Rose unlatched the wooden door of the chicken coop, closed it behind her, and leaned down. She and her sisters had raised most of the chickens by hand, and the others were just as tame. Each of the hens had their own distinct personality. She picked each one up and gave them a cuddle as she spoke to them softly. When she remembered her mother was waiting on the eggs, she stood up.

"How many eggs do you have for us this morning?" she asked as she looked in the straw bedding. She found eight eggs when there were normally twelve to fifteen every morning. Rose had a better look around and found two more.

"Better than nothing," she said aloud. "*Denke*, my little friends."

Leaving the basket of eggs by the door, she freshened their water and topped up their grain. She looked at the straw and wondered if she should change that too, but left that to Tulip.

"Well, that took you long enough," her mother said when Rose got back to the house.

Rose placed the wicker basket of eggs on the table.

"Don't put them there. The basket's dirty. Put it on the floor. You should know these things by now. Why can't you remember anything?"

"Sorry, *Mamm*." Rose obeyed her mother and placed the basket on the floor. She then proceeded to put the eggs in the ceramic bowl where they were kept, on the counter by the sink.

Her twin sisters suddenly appeared and sat down at the table, while Tulip was nowhere to be seen.

"*Mamm* says you've got to get married." Daisy, the older of the twins, laughed.

"Do you think you'll find someone with your head on fire like that?" Lily added.

The twins giggled. They always poked fun at her red hair. Their hair was dark, as was everyone else's in their family. Two generations ago, she'd been told, there were some red-haired family members, but Rose was the only one of this generation to have that color.

"That's not very nice," their mother reprimanded the twins. "And you know you shouldn't be eavesdropping. I won't warn you again."

"Sorry, *Mamm*," the twins said in unison.

"Your turn is coming," Rose said to her sisters.

"I want to be married soon, and I'll have three sets of twins and then no more," Lily said.

Daisy gave a laugh, and said, "Me too. I'll have one set of girls, one set of boys, then more girls. Then I'm done too. There'll be fewer childbirths and pregnancies if I have all my *kinner* in sets of twins."

"What about triplets?" Lily asked her sister, which made Daisy giggle.

"So, who are you going to marry?" Rose asked them.

"I rather not talk about it," Daisy replied.

"What about you, Lily?" Rose figured she'd do some teasing of her own.

"Forget about us. You're the oldest *dochder*, Rose. Who are you going to marry?" Daisy stared at her. "That's more important right now. You are the one who has to set the example because you're the eldest. Isn't that right, *Mamm*?"

"I expect Rose to marry first but it doesn't have to be that way."

"Well, who's it going to be?" Lily asked Rose.

"You'll just have to wait and see."

"She's got no idea," Daisy said to Lily.

When both twins laughed, it was too much for Rose. "Make them stop, *Mamm*."

"We're going to wash the windows today," their mother announced to the twins.

Both sisters groaned and Rose couldn't help but giggle. She had a nice little job working at the farmers market. She ran a flower stall for the Walkers, an Amish family, who owned a wholesale flower business. They also had a small stall at the farmers market, which Rose ran for them.

A job was far better than staying home every day, cooking, or scrubbing the house from top to bottom. And to make matters worse for her sisters, their mother always insisted on things being just so. With Rose having no horse and buggy of her own, Mrs. Walker collected Rose every day and also brought her home. This suited Mrs. Walker because after she took Rose to the market, she'd continue to her elderly mother's house and stay with her to help until the workday was done. It was also convenient that the Walkers lived right next door.

After breakfast, Rose grabbed her black shawl off the peg by the back door and yelled goodbye to everyone.

"Come here, Rose."

"*Jah*, what is it, *Mamm*? Do you want me to bring something home with me?"

"*Nee.*" Her mother hurried over to her and said, quietly, "I want you to spend the day thinking about what men you might like to marry. When you get home, we'll discuss them one by one."

"I can't, *Mamm*. I'll need time to think. Can I take a few weeks to think about it?" Rose bit her lip. "What if the man I'm supposed to marry doesn't even live in this community?"

Her mother's eyes opened wide. It was clearly something that her mother had never considered. "That wouldn't do at all. I think he'll be from around here somewhere. There are many to choose from, but you mustn't delay. This time next year, many of the single men will be spoken for. If you wait, you'll end up without."

Her mother's words sent a chill down her spine. The thought of ending up with no one to marry was something Rose had never considered. Surely God would put couples together without it being a race. "I'll definitely give it some serious thought, *Mamm*."

"*Gut* girl. We'll talk more about it tonight."

Rose nodded, knowing her mother only wanted the best for her.

She walked down the driveway listening to the crunch of the small white pebbles underneath her black lace-up boots.

At the end of the drive, she leaned against the gate-post and waited for her ride. Mornings were Rose's favorite time of the day. She loved to watch the birds going about their work gathering small twigs and other odds and ends to make their nests, and plucking the occasional worm from the soft earth. It was spring and everything seemed fresh and new.

Once she saw Mrs. Walker's gray horse trotting toward her, she took some steps closer to the road, so she could get in quickly before the buggy would slow any passing traffic. Traffic was something they rarely saw down their road apart from the occasional weekend tourist looking at the countryside, but Rose was still careful.

"How are you this morning, Rose?" Mrs. Walker asked as soon as she stopped on the side of the road.

"Fine, *Denke*. What about yourself?"

"I'll feel better when it rains."

"*Jah*, it hasn't rained for some time and we surely need it."

Every morning one of the Walkers' sons got to the market early and loaded the stall with fresh flowers. All Rose had to do was arrange them nicely and, of course, sell them.

"Your *bruder* and Amy were very happy to be getting married," Mrs. Walker commented.

"*Jah, Dat* said they were made for each other."

"It certainly looks that way."

Rose was tempted to talk more about the wedding, but she didn't want to let on that her mother had given her what was close to an ultimatum about getting married within one year. Mrs. Walker had two sons who were single and Rose didn't want Mrs. Walker to think that she was hinting about one of her sons.

"How old were you when you got married, Mrs. Walker?"

"It was the day after I turned eighteen. Our parents made us wait to get married. We grew up together, right next door—side-by-side. We always knew we were going to marry each other."

"That must've been very comforting—knowing where your destiny lay."

"*Jah.* I always knew we would be together, and he knew it too." Mrs. Walker glanced at her. "What about you? Do you have a boy you're interested in?"

"*Nee*, not really."

"That sounds a bit doubtful. Have you got your eyes on someone?"

Laughter escaped Rose's lips. "I wish I did; then things might be easier for me."

"There's no rush; you're still young."

Tell my mother that, she thought. "That's true."

Mrs. Walker prattled on about what flowers were going to be at the stall that morning. "And the daisies aren't looking as fresh as they should be, so you can mark them down or give people more for their money. You know what to do."

"I do." Rose had to agree. If there was one thing she knew how to do, it was to sell flowers. She knew when they weren't looking their best and then the aim was to mark them down in price enough so they'd sell that day. It was better to get a little money before they wilted too far. The Walkers didn't freeze their flowers like many of the other flower wholesalers did, so the shelf life was considerably less. Fortunately, there had been a strong demand for local produce. Retail florists were favoring locally grown flowers, which helped the Walker family.

Chapter Three

Blessed is that man that maketh the Lord his trust,
and respecteth not the proud, nor such as turn
aside to lies.

Psalm 40:4

At work that day, Rose's mother's words played through her mind.

Since he had no customers Mark took a few steps toward Rose. "What's got you so upset, Rosie?"

She looked into Mark's concerned face. "Who said I'm upset? I'm not, not at all."

"Maybe upset's the wrong word, but something's on your mind. Tell me what it is?"

She stared at the pink roses in the bucket by her feet, and answered, "It's nothing."

"It must be something."

Looking back at Mark, she said, "*Nee*, it's not."

"Tell me." He put his hands on his hips and stared at her, narrowing his eyes.

"It's just that I feel under pressure. Now that my *mudder* has got my two brothers married off, she's turning her attention to me. She tells me I must *plan* to be married by next year."

"Plan?" He chuckled. "Or what?"

"She didn't exactly say what would happen if I wasn't married by then. I think she is worried that I'll never get married if it doesn't happen by then, or something." Rose shrugged her shoulders.

"Rosie, if you want to marry me, just say it. You don't have to make up a story about something your *mudder* said."

She stared into Mark's smiling face. If only life were as simple as Mark made it out to be. "Ha ha, very funny."

"I'm sorry to be unsympathetic. Who does your *mudder* think you should marry? Has she got some man lined up for you?"

"She wants me to give her some names tonight. I've got today to think about it."

Mark roared with laughter.

"Don't laugh."

"Maybe I should pay your *mudder* a call, and tell her I'm the man for you. She should know that already."

"Don't you dare!"

"You could do worse."

"Is that the best reason you can come up with for me to marry you—the fact that I could do worse?"

"I suppose not. I'll make a list of my good points and present them to Mrs. Yoder next time I see her. Perhaps I should stop by for dinner one night?" He tapped on his chin with his finger and looked upward. "I hope she is considering me for the job."

"I'm quite serious about this; it could become quite a problem. You know what my *mudder* is like when she gets her mind set on something."

"I don't know personally, but you've told me, so I have to take your word for that."

"I've got customers heading this way." Rose served some of her regular customers while Mark stayed behind his stall.

Mark ran a cheese stall at the end of the food line, and Rose's stall shared the corner of his where the flowers aisle started. Mark's family had a goat farm and made goat cheeses and other related products. The most popular products were the goats' milk and cheese. Mark had spent many an hour telling Rose how much better goats' milk was than cows' milk, mainly because it was easier to digest.

As the day drew to a close, Mark walked over to Rose. "I've come up with a plan for you."

"A plan to do what?"

"If your *mudder* gets too high-pressured, we can always pretend that we're dating. You and me."

Rose considered what he said before she answered. "It might work for a while. Then she'll put pressure on us at the end of the year to marry."

He raised his eyebrows. "The offer's there."

"How do you see it would work? My *mudder's* not easily fooled. She's a very smart woman."

"It would take the focus off you if she thinks you've already got someone lined up to possibly marry. She could turn her energy onto one of your sisters."

Rose giggled. "It seems like a good plan. *Denke*, I'll definitely give it some thought."

Mark smiled, and then turned back to securing his stall for the night. He'd never made a secret of liking her. Rose knew she'd only have to say the word and they'd be dating. But Mark was just a friend and Rose couldn't see herself marrying him. He was just a shade taller and he was an ordinary looking man. Rose had always known how she'd feel about her husband when she first laid eyes on him. There would be tingles running up and down her spine, and her heart would pitter-patter when he came close. He'd be tall, with dark eyes and dark hair, with olive tanned skin and dazzling white teeth.

Yes, she'd recognize him when she saw him, and that's something she'd always known in her heart. Rose hadn't met the man she'd share her life with. Perhaps her mother was right and she couldn't waste time. Her future husband was out there somewhere and she had to find him soon before he married another. What if his mother was also putting pressure on him to marry? He might marry someone else before they found each other.

Chapter Four

Thou hast turned for me my mourning into dancing:
thou hast put off my sackcloth, and girded me with
gladness;

Psalm 30:11

Nancy Yoder looked out the window to see Rose walking toward the house. Rose was a sweet girl, and nothing but a dreamer. If she didn't set the girl on the right path, what would become of her?

Rose was a tall and willowy girl, attractive with her brilliant red hair, but that would do her no good if she didn't get her head in the right space—and fast. Nancy had been blessed to find her husband when she was a young teenager, but if Rose didn't think about finding a man now, it might be too late. She could see in Rose's eyes from earlier that day she'd felt the pressure of her words. Rose was a girl who needed guidance, and besides, it was for her own good that she marry soon.

"Tulip, take your sisters upstairs. I want to have a word with Rose alone before your *vadder* gets home."

"*Mamm*, we're not three-years-old," Daisy said.

"Yeah! We don't need anyone to take us upstairs." Lily jumped to her feet.

"We'll go by ourselves, *Mamm*," Tulip added in a tone of disgust.

Tulip never liked to be grouped with the twins preferring to be treated as older along with Rose. Her three younger daughters made themselves scarce, while Nancy waited by the door for Rose.

When Rose pushed the door open, her mother was right in front of her.

"*Mamm!* Where is everyone?"

"The girls are upstairs. Sit down with me for a moment so we can talk alone."

Rose studied her mother's face to carefully judge her mood while she let the shawl slide from her shoulders. "Have I done something wrong?"

"*Nee*. I want to talk more about what I was saying this morning."

Rose hung her shawl on the peg behind the door, and walked into the living room. She sat on the couch and her mother sat down next to her.

Nancy inhaled deeply. "Rose, I know you think I'm meddling in your life, but I don't want you to have regrets about anything when you're older."

"I'm only twenty."

Nancy felt bad that she hadn't had this conversation with Rose two years ago. There had been many men who had gotten married in those years, and five of them she could name off the top of her head, any one of whom might've been perfect for her daughter.

"If you don't act now to find a husband—"

"I'll miss out," Rose finished her sentence for her while nodding her head.

"*Jah*, you will. Now, you said you'd give it some thought today, so did you think of anyone you might like?" Nancy watched as Rose's eyes glazed over. "Perhaps I should get your *vadder* to talk to you?"

"*Nee, Mamm. Dat* wouldn't be comfortable talking about things like this."

"Well?"

"I… I have thought about it and…"

Nancy leaned forward placing her fingertips behind her ear to pull her ear forward. It was something she used to do when her children were smaller to show them that she was listening intently. Old habits were hard to break. "And?"

"And I do like someone, but we've been keeping it quiet."

Keeping relationships quiet was often the Amish way among the young. Many people didn't know couples were together until their weddings were published, and a date for the wedding announced.

Nancy was relieved. "You have? You like someone and he likes you in return?"

Rose nodded. "That's right."

"Who is it?"

"If I tell you, it won't be keeping it quiet."

Nancy nodded. Rose had the right to privacy because she was an adult now and Nancy had to respect her rights. Still, Nancy hated it when there was something she didn't know. Who was this mystery man? Was he a suitable match? The thing that kept Nancy awake at night was that Rose was a girl who could easily be led astray. The girl just didn't think things through. Or was the whole thing a ruse made up by Rose to deflect attention and put off finding a man? "Perhaps we could have him over for dinner one night?"

Rose bit her lip. "Maybe."

"Rose, are you just saying this to stop me talking to you about marriage? Does this man exist other than in your daydreams?"

"*Mamm*, how could you possibly say that to me?"

"You're not denying it. This morning you made no mention of this man and that would've been the opportunity to do so. Why's that? Why didn't you talk about your man this morning?"

Rose crossed her arms over her chest and slumped back into the couch. "He does exist."

"Then who is he?"

"I don't want to make a big deal out of it. Can't we just leave it at that? I'll take notice of your warnings about finding myself missing out if I wait too long."

"Do I know him?"

"Of course you do. He's from our community. I'm not sneaking off to see an *Englischer*. You should at least be happy about that."

From Rose's response, it was more clear Rose knew Nancy wouldn't be happy about her choice in a man.

She thought about all the men she'd seen Rose with over the past weeks and the only man she could think of was Mark Schumacher. The two of them were always talking together to the exclusion of others. She closed her eyes picturing them as a couple, and in the future, married. Then she opened them and locked eyes with Rose. "Mark Schumacher?"

"Why do you say it like that?"

"I'm just asking you a question. Is that who the mystery man is?"

"*Jah*, it's Mark, and there's nothing wrong with him."

"*Nee*, there isn't. I like Mark."

Rose sat on her hands. "You do?"

"*Jah.* He's a fine young man. And you clearly get along with one another."

"Please don't make a big fuss of it. I don't want you to scare him away."

Nancy laughed, trying to hide her amazement. Mark was an unusual choice. In her mind's eye, she'd always imagined Rose with someone older; someone who would act as a stabilizing influence on her. Mark was barely a year older than she. And, what's more, Mark struck Nancy as someone who seemed a little casual in his approach to life.

Then, another thought troubled Nancy. What if Mark was merely her first boyfriend and she'd grow tired of him? He would distract her, waste her time, and when their relationship was done, she'd be older and many of the men would've already married. She looked back at her daughter. "Are you sure about Mark?"

"Don't worry; we won't be getting married tomorrow." Rose laughed.

That wasn't what Nancy was concerned about, but she didn't want to worry Rose with her own troubling doubts since Rose was prone to nerves and anxiety. Rose had been better these past years, but any added stress on her oldest daughter wouldn't be good.

Nancy knew she'd have to let it go as best she could, and trust God. Rose was seeing someone and even if she thought him not a good fit for her, she reminded herself that it was Rose's choice.

"Have I upset you or something, *Mamm*?"

She stared into her daughter's bright green eyes that perfectly complemented the red tones of her crowning glory. Without saying a word, she leaned forward and kissed her daughter on her forehead. "You couldn't possibly upset me."

Chapter Five

For his anger endureth but a moment; in his favour is life: weeping may endure for a night, but joy cometh in the morning.

Psalm 30:5

Rose was taken aback. Her *mudder* was not one for physical affection with her grown children. She watched her mother stand and hurry into the kitchen.

Over her shoulder *Mamm* called out, "Can you let your sisters know we've finished our talk?"

Sisters? Where are they? Still sitting, Rose leaned over to look up the stairs. Moving shadows proved that they had been listening in. Rose quietly bounded to her feet and caught sight of them. "I see you!"

The twins giggled and ran down the stairs while pushing and shoving each other.

"We heard *Mamm* say we could come down now." Lily stuck her nose in the air as she sailed past Rose.

Daisy was right behind Lily and poked out her tongue at Rose when she walked by.

Rose ignored her and looked back up the stairs wondering where Tulip was. "You up there, Tulip?"

Tulip appeared. "Yeah."

Rose knew that Tulip was so gentle and polite that she didn't want to let on that she'd been listening along with the twins. "You heard?"

"I did." Her face twisted with guilt.

"It's okay."

Tulip walked down toward her. With Rose's best friend having left the community to go on *rumspringa*, Tulip had become her closest female friend.

"Is it true about Mark?"

Rose gulped. If Tulip didn't believe her, that meant her mother would also have doubts. "Not really."

"Then why did you say that to *Mamm*?"

"Are you two helping or what?" rang the raucous voice of one of the twins from the kitchen.

"We're coming in a minute," Rose yelled back.

"Well? I know it's not true," Tulip said.

Rose sighed. "I had to do something. *Mamm* told me I need to get married soon, but there's no one around for me to marry. She was putting me under pressure."

"Why don't we visit some relatives in other towns— just you and me? That way, we can meet more people and you might find someone."

"I'm not in a hurry. And I can't leave the stall. Mr. and Mrs. Walker need me."

"Someone else would be able to do it for a while. Think about it. It'll look like you're doing something to find a man and we can have a good time together."

"I can't. If I do that, *Mamm* will know that I lied to her and I'll never hear the end of it."

"She'll find out soon enough, won't she?"

"*Nee*. I hope not."

"You roped Mark into the lie with you?"

Rose cringed at the word 'lie.' "You make it sound

as though it's something terrible." It was best to keep it to herself that Mark was the one who'd come up with the idea.

Tulip shook her head and her prayer *kapp* strings were thrown side-to-side. "This won't end well."

"Maybe and maybe not, but can't we keep this between the two of us?" Rose whispered.

Tulip nodded and the pair joined the others in the kitchen to help prepare the evening meal.

Later that evening, Nancy was in her bedroom with her husband.

"Did you have a talk with Rose?" Hezekiah asked.

"About her getting married?"

"Jah."

"I did, and she says that she and Mark Schumacher have been seeing quite a bit of each other."

He drew his head back in surprise. "Besides seeing each other every day at the farmers market?"

"Jah, it seems so. She's fond of him."

Scratching his neck, he asked, "Do you think she's taking things more seriously now since your talk?"

"Maybe. I don't like to put pressure on the girl, but she's twenty now. I would've hoped she would have found someone before now, but it seems she wasn't seriously looking," Nancy said. "She must not have been taking her relationship with Mark seriously."

"We don't always know what's going on in our *kinners'* lives."

"Jah, especially when they get older. I just hope my talk didn't put too much pressure on her. You know what she's like."

"You did the right thing, Nancy. There's pressure in

life and we can't escape that. She'll have to learn to deal with it."

"I suppose so, but I always feel overprotective, more protective of Rose than our other *kinner*. She's the sensitive one, while Tulip is the smart one. The twins—"

"The twins will mature in time." Hezekiah smiled as he often did when the twins were mentioned.

"What do you think of Mark?"

"He's a nice boy."

"Exactly! A boy. He's not a man really, is he?" Nancy asked. "He's just a freckle-faced boy. I can't see him being a man and taking care of our Rose."

"He's still young—give him a chance."

Nancy's gaze swept upward to the ceiling. "I always saw Rose with someone older."

Hezekiah chuckled. "And he will be older in a few years. Stop worrying so much. Things have a way of following their natural course. She just needs to relax and the current of life will set her on the right course."

Nancy looked into her husband's eyes and was comforted. Maybe she was being overly concerned. She wanted Rose to be interested in a man, and now she'd found out she had something going on with Mark. He was an interesting choice and she'd have to keep a close eye on the two of them.

Chapter Six

O Lord, thou hast brought up my soul from the grave: thou hast kept me alive, that I should not go down to the pit.

Psalm 30:3

Rose couldn't wait to get to work to tell Mark that she'd taken him up on his offer of him being her pretend love-interest. As soon as Mrs. Walker dropped her off at the entrance of the farmers market, she hurried to their side-by-side stalls.

Mark had his back turned so she grabbed him by his arm and pulled him behind the stalls so no one would hear what she said.

"Whooaa! What are you doing, Rosie?"

"I need to tell you something important," Rose whispered.

"What is it?" He leaned forward and opened his eyes wide.

"It's my *mudder*—you know what we were talking about yesterday afternoon?"

"*Jah?*"

"I had to pretend that you were my boyfriend."

Mark appeared to be enjoying every moment of Rose's dilemma. A hint of smugness touched his lips as he leaned back on one foot and crossed his arms in front of his chest. Then he straightened up. "Hang on a minute. You're not joking with me?"

"*Nee.* I'm telling you what happened and what I had to say to *Mamm.*"

He sighed and rubbed his chin. "Tell me what happened. Tell me everything—who said what?"

"I was frightened she might send me away somewhere or try to find someone for me." Rose imagined what kind of man her mother would find for her. Probably someone old and stuffy who never laughed, who had a big farm somewhere, and would come home smelly and sweaty at the end of the day. "Anyway, it's all right, isn't it? It was you who suggested the whole thing."

"It was a joke, Rose. I wasn't serious."

Rose opened her mouth in surprise. "*Nee*, it was not a joke! You can't say this to me now, Mark. I more or less already told my *mudder* that you're my boyfriend."

"I wasn't serious. How do you think we'd ever pull that off?"

"I haven't thought it through, obviously. My *mudder* put me on the spot and then I just kept hearing your voice repeat what you said yesterday." She shook her head. "I can't believe you're letting me down when the whole thing was entirely your idea."

He rubbed his chin not looking as smug as he had a moment before. "Are you blaming me for this whole thing, Rosie?"

"*Jah*, I am. I'm totally blaming you for everything. All of it. It was all your idea and now you're leaving me hanging. I'll look so foolish when I tell *Mamm* I made it all up." Rose huffed and folded her arms across her chest.

Mark shrugged his shoulders. "I'll go along with it, if it'll get you out of a jam." One side of his mouth tilted into a crooked smile.

"*Denke*, Mark, you're a lifesaver." She leaned forward and gave him a quick kiss on his cheek.

When she pulled her head away, he put his fingers where she'd kissed him.

"Now, about my benefits for pretending to be your boyfriend." His eyes sparkled with mischief.

"You'll simply do this as a friend—as a favor to help me. There'll be no payments made or benefits of any kind. Agreed? And we're only acting; this is not real. Okay?"

He rubbed his forehead and breathed out heavily. "Agreed. The things I get myself into. How well do we have to act this thing out?"

"Just long enough to fool my parents for as long as my *mudder* has this bug in her head about me marrying. It will probably pass in a couple of weeks. I'm sure it's just because of Trevor's wedding."

"Just a couple of weeks, eh?"

"I'm sure that's all it'll take. Anyway, this is all your fault, so don't pull that face."

"How could it be my fault? I'm not the one who wants to trick her *mudder*."

"You should've just kept your mouth closed because if you hadn't said—"

"Okay, okay—lesson learned. I agree with you. Next time I'll shut my—"

"Hi, Rose."

Rose turned to see one of the Walker boys, who was delivering more flowers to the stall.

"Hello, Sam." Rose left Mark so she could instruct Sam where she wanted the flowers placed.

When Sam had delivered the last bucket off the trolley, he hung around talking for longer than usual. Rose thought it a little odd and wondered whether her mother was matchmaking already and had spoken to Sam about her. And if that was so, it meant *Mamm* didn't believe the story about Mark. Rose knew Sam had a second job to get to. He worked with his parents in the morning, and then worked for a building company throughout the day.

When Sam left, Mark walked over. "Were you trying to make your pretend boyfriend jealous just now?"

"Did it work?"

He laughed. "Not really."

"Well, you'll need more practice as a boyfriend. Am I your first girlfriend?"

"First pretend one." He laughed and went back to straightening his stall ready for the day's customers.

Rose's mind danced around Mark and the memories of him for as far back as she could recall. She'd never heard about Mark having a girlfriend and she was convinced he'd never had one.

It was the middle of the day when Rose saw a dreadful sight. Her mother was walking toward her with the twins dawdling along behind.

Rose stopped and stared, waiting for them to get close. This wasn't good. She was only there to see the interaction between herself and Mark. What other reason would she have for being there? "*Mamm*, what are you doing here? I could've brought something home for you."

"*Nee*, I'm just looking around to see what I can see." She turned her head looking at nothing in particular, in a false manner, until she caught Mark's eye. Then she waved to him. "Mark, it's so nice to see you again."

"*Jah*, we haven't seen each other since—it must have been as long ago as last week!"

Her mother giggled. "You're always full of jokes, Mark."

"Not always," Mark answered.

"Why don't you come over for dinner tomorrow night, Mark? We'd love to have you there."

He pointed to himself as his eyes bugged. "Me?"

"*Jah*, you. I can't remember that we've ever had you to the *haus* apart from when we have the Sunday meetings there."

Rose's heart skipped a beat. As Mark stammered a response, he glanced at Rose who was trying to hide behind her mother. Meanwhile, Rose's two youngest sisters were talking to each other, unaware of what was going on around them.

"I… I… I'd love to. *Denke*, Mrs. Yoder."

"I'll look forward to it. Mr. Yoder and I can get to know you better." Nancy turned to her eldest daughter. "I'll see you tonight, Rose."

When Nancy and the twins were in the distance, Rose said to Mark, who was also staring after them, "This is a disaster."

"Not really. It's only dinner."

"Don't you see? She didn't believe me and now she wants to question you."

"She didn't believe that you and I are in love?"

"I didn't say we were in love. I kind of just made out that we have been on a couple of dates."

"Did we enjoy them?"

"Mark, you agreed to do this for me. Don't give me a hard time about it."

"Don't worry about things. Everything will go smoothly. You're over-thinking things, besides I'm a good actor. If you and I are dating, they want to see what kind of person I am. That's only normal. My parents would do the same—I think—if I were a female and you were my pretend boyfriend. Going on that scenario, you'd have to be a man, which would be kinda weird." He scratched his head. "Weirder still, me being female…"

Despite Mark's assurances and nonsense babbling, Rose knew what she'd said previously was true. "This is dreadful."

"What did you think would happen, Rosie? This is part of it—part of us pretending to be a couple." He shook his head, looking serious, with lines appearing on his normally smooth forehead.

Rose knew Mark was worried and trying his best to hide it. There was no other way but to go through with it. It was better they believed Mark was her boyfriend rather than have them pushing her onto someone else.

"I guess it might go okay tonight."

He smiled. "Now you're talking. Don't worry so much."

"I just hope they don't ask you any hard questions."

"If they do, I'll answer them."

Even if Mark was nervous, his confident words gave Rose a slight amount of comfort.

The next two hours passed by quickly, with many customers keeping the two of them busy.

Then, just as Rose pulled a sandwich out of her lunch-box, she saw him striding her way. He was a large young Amish man in a billowing white shirt, and nicely tailored black pants held up by black suspenders.

Chapter Seven

*He delivereth me from mine enemies: yea, thou
liftest me up above those that rise up against me:
thou hast delivered me from the violent man.*

Psalm 18:48

Rose rubbed her eyes and looked at the Amish man
heading toward her.

He was as she'd always imagined he would be. He
carried himself with a confidence unlike the regular
Amish men from her community. Her sandwich dropped
from her hands and she dusted off the crumbs, all the
while watching to see which way he went.

On he walked, directly toward her. To her absolute
delight, he was clean-shaven signifying he was a single
man. This had to be her future husband; she could feel it
in every part of her body. Did he know it too? He smiled
at her when he stopped in front of Mark's stall. To Rose,
it was as though she'd waited all her life for this moment.

He turned his attention to Mark and Rose heard him
whisper, "Do you know who that girl is?" He then nodded his head subtly in her direction.

Who was the man? Mark knew him, that was clear.

Clearing his throat, Mark moved away from behind his stall and closer to Rose. "Rose, come over and meet my cousin."

Rose took a few steps toward him. It was when she was closer that the warm sunlight lit up his eyes and she saw the flecks of amber in the brown eyes that gazed back at her.

"Nice to meet you…" She glanced over at Mark hoping Mark would say his cousin's name.

The handsome stranger took her hand in his. His hand was large, warm, and easily covered hers.

"I'm Jacob."

"Hello, Jacob."

"Hello, Rose," he said, still staring into her eyes.

"Where are you from?" Rose asked, amazed she could find her voice.

"I'm from Oakes County. I'm visiting for a few weeks, learning how to build buggies from Mark's and my *onkel* Harry."

That was the best news Rose had heard for a long time. He released her hand and she dropped it by her side, still looking at him. She wanted to know more about the handsome stranger, but she couldn't think what else to ask.

"Is this your stall?" Jacob nodded his head toward the flowers.

"It's not mine, but I watch it. I look after it for the Walkers."

"Rose's flower stall," he said grinning.

He wasn't the first person to comment on her name in connection to the flower stall.

She looked down at her feet and shuffled them. "I know. It's a funny thing."

Mark interrupted them. "Rose's mother named all her

daughters after flowers. There's Rose, as you know, then there are Tulip, and the twins, Lily and Daisy."

"That's delightful."

"Rose's aunty, that would be her *mudder's schweschder*, has two *kinner* and also called them after flowers. That made Rose's *mudder* angry and now Mrs. Yoder doesn't speak to her younger *schweschder* anymore—that would be Rose's aunt."

Rose frowned at Mark wondering why he was jabbering on about things she'd told him in the strictest confidence. "Mark!"

Mark cleared his throat and appeared not to care in the slightest that he'd revealed something so sensitive. "Are you here to deliver a message to me or something, Jacob?"

Jacob frowned. "*Nee*, I just wanted to have a look around while I'm here." His face brightened when he turned back to Rose. "It would be good if I could find someone who knew the area to show me around."

From the way he smiled, Rose knew he was dropping a large hint. She wasted no time in responding. "I could show you around sometime if you'd like." This was an opportunity too good to allow to slip away.

"I'd like that very much."

"*Gut!* I'll drive us," Mark said. "You don't have your buggy here, Jacob, and Rose doesn't have a buggy of her own."

Rose's mouth dropped open and she stared at Mark. Why was he trying to ruin things for her? He was acting like they were dating for real.

"I'm sure I could borrow a buggy while I'm here," Jacob said as he looked down on his cousin. He was a good six inches taller than Mark.

Mark frowned. "Rose and I are…"

"*Ah*, I'm sorry." Jacob raised both hands in the air and took a step back. "I didn't realize. I had no idea."

"*Nee*, it's not like that," Rose shot back.

Mark swiveled his head and stared at Rose. He looked hurt; she could see it in his eyes, but at that moment, Rose couldn't let Jacob think that she was taken.

"I can show you around. Mark and I are only friends," Rose assured him. "And nothing more," she added for good measure.

"Enough said, Rose!" Mark raised his voice. "I'll work out a time with you tonight, Jacob. Tomorrow night, I'm having dinner at Rose's *haus.* Maybe you could arrange something for Saturday afternoon?"

"Sounds good." Jacob turned to Rose. "I'll see you again soon, Rose."

Rose smiled, but was too upset to speak. Mark had picked the worst time to be so bossy. She'd never seen him like that and neither had she known him to raise his voice in that manner.

As soon as Jacob was gone, Rose knew she needed to find out what had been going through Mark's mind. "Why did you do that? We aren't really dating! You acted like a jealous boyfriend and embarrassed me in front of your cousin."

"It was you who talked me into this, Rose. I have to go to your parents' *haus* tomorrow, have dinner with you all, and pretend we're in some kind of a relationship. How am I going to do that if we tell some people we aren't and some we are?" He shook his head. "I don't like being in a position like this. I respect your parents and I don't like lying to them. Now we'll both be found out, for sure and for certain."

Rose didn't know what to say. He had a point. Her father had always told her that no good came from dishonesty. Now she was learning her lesson in the worst way possible. If she hadn't made up the lie about Mark and herself dating, she would have been able to be alone with Jacob without Mark getting in the way. She glanced over at Mark who was still fuming. "I'm sorry. I didn't think the whole thing through."

"We've got to stick to the story, Rosie. What do you want the story to be? You can go home today and tell your parents we ended things today if that's what you want. You tell me what you want to tell them and I'll go along with it."

If she did as he suggested, there was no guarantee that Mark's cousin was just as taken with her as she was with him, but she had to try. Otherwise, Jacob might slip right through her fingers. He was the only man she'd ever been attracted to.

"Okay. I'll tell them that we thought it best to end things."

He raised his eyebrows indicating he'd expected a different response. He nodded, and then turned away without saying a word.

Typical man, sulking, she thought. It would've suited Mark to pretend they were boyfriend and girlfriend, so he could be closer to her more often. After she'd given him time to cool down, she said, "I'm sorry, Mark."

He looked over at her. "For what?"

"To drag you into my silly schemes."

He laughed. "It wasn't all your fault. It was my stupid idea. I'm telling you right now you should never listen to anything I say."

"And why did you tell him all that private stuff about the spat my *mudder* is having with Aunt Nerida?"

"It's a little more than a spat. Spat's are over quickly. This has been going on for years." Rose frowned at him, until he said, "I know; I'm sorry. It came out without me thinking."

"Obviously! It was clear you weren't thinking." Rose shook her head.

"To make things up to you, why don't you come to dinner one night at my parents' *haus* while Jacob's here?"

"He's staying with you?"

"*Jah*, right there in the *haus.*"

He knew she liked Jacob. She didn't want to hurt Mark's feelings, but she was never going to marry Mark and he had to come to terms with that. She didn't want to lead him on in any way. "I'd like that, *denke.*"

"Tell your parents about our demise tonight, adding that we're still friends and you're coming over to my *haus* for dinner tomorrow night instead of me going over there. If that's okay with your *mudder.*"

"It will be. *Denke.* I'll do that."

"You might as well bring Tulip with you and that will look more believable."

That last part wasn't a good idea. *What if Jacob fancies Tulip before he gets to know me? I can't risk it.* "I can ask her. She might not come along."

He shrugged. "Suit yourself. If you want to, you can come home with me tomorrow night from here. Unless you need to go home to pretty yourself up, or something—not that you need to."

Rose giggled. "I'll let Mrs. Walker know she won't need to take me home tomorrow night."

The rest of the day flew by and Rose couldn't wait to get home so she could tell Tulip all about Jacob, the man her instincts told her she would marry one day.

Rose usually arrived home when everyone was preparing dinner and this night was no different. She walked into the kitchen hoping to have a private moment with her mother to tell her that things were over with Mark. Her mother looked up when she walked into the room.

"There you are. Can you set the table?"

"Sure."

The twins were chattering amongst themselves while Tulip was busy making dessert. Rose opened the cutlery drawer and pulled out knives and forks. "Can I talk with you for a quick moment in the lounge room, *Mamm*?"

Her mother swung around and looked at her. "Right now?"

"*Jah.*"

"Lily, you're setting the table now."

Lily scowled as Rose handed her the knives and forks.

When Rose and her mother sat down on the couch in the living room, her mother started the conversation. "Is everything all right, Rose?"

"Everything is fine, but Mark and I decided to end things. It's regrettable, but that's how things turned out in the end." She placed her hands in her lap and tried to look a little forlorn.

Her mother leaned back and her eyebrows drew together. "Over before they even began?"

"Well, they began and then they ended."

"The whole thing doesn't seem believable, Rose."

"Mark and I decided we are more suited to be friends than anything else. And we decided to remain just that— friends. It would've been a big mistake if we'd continued our relationship."

"Well, that is disappointing. I really like Mark."

"That's not what you said yesterday."

Her mother's mouth contracted into a straight line. "What I said was that I've always liked Mark. I distinctly remember that."

"It's probably not what you said, but how you said it. I got the feeling you thought we weren't suited."

"It's what you think that counts, Rose."

"Is that what you truly believe, *Mamm*?"

"Of course it is."

"*Gut* because today, I met someone I really like. He's someone who's staying with Mark." She twirled one of the strings of her prayer *kapp* between her fingers as visions of Jacob came into her mind.

"Who is it?"

"Mark's cousin. His name is Jacob. He's come here to learn to make buggies from Harry. I think he might only be here for a few weeks."

"That is very awkward for you, Rose."

"Why?"

"Because of Mark."

"Not really."

"They're cousins."

"Oh, I see what you mean. Mark and I are such good friends that Mark invited me over to dinner tomorrow night and, well, he said if that's all right with you. It wouldn't be right for him to come over for dinner because we aren't a couple anymore and that's why you invited Mark."

"What you're saying is instead of Mark coming here for dinner tomorrow night for your *vadder* and me to get to know him better, you're having dinner at his place because you like his cousin and you're no longer interested in Mark?"

Rose carefully considered what her mother said. "*Jah.*"

Her mother tipped her head to one side. "It all sounds very suspicious. Are you sure you're telling me everything?"

"I'm not keeping anything from you, if that's what you mean." At that moment there was a loud crash in the kitchen.

"I hope that wasn't the roast," Rose's mother called out to her daughters in the kitchen.

"It was just Tulip being clumsy again," Lily called out which caused an argument in the kitchen between the three girls.

"As long as you know what you're doing, Rose."

"I do. I really like Jacob."

"But that's the thing I don't understand. You told me there was no one, and then suddenly there was Mark, and now Mark is finished then on the very same day Jacob appears." Her mother wagged a finger at her. "I know I'm not getting the full story here."

When the argument got louder, her mother stood up and headed to the kitchen. "We haven't finished talking about this, Rose," she said over her shoulder.

"That's fine, but can I go to Mark's for dinner tomorrow night? It's all been arranged."

"Okay, but I'll have to ask your *vadder* first. I'm not going to bother him with it until after dinner."

Rose was relieved. Even though her mother didn't quite believe her, Rose was certain her father would allow her to go to dinner. That meant only twenty-four hours to wait before she could see Jacob again.

After dinner that night, Tulip lay across Rose's bed on her stomach with her chin cupped in her palms while listening to Rose tell again how handsome Jacob was.

"He's so tall, and his eyes are like dark liquid amber. They are dark with amber flecks."

"Brown eyes?" Tulip asked.

"Brown, but with flecks of gold. He looked at me,

and I knew he felt something too. He even asked Mark about me. I heard him."

"Where was Mark?"

Mark? Rose was reminded she still hadn't gotten the full permission to go to dinner tomorrow night. She needed both her parents' approval.

"I feel bad about telling *Mamm* that I was dating Mark. It was a stupid thing to do."

"There's no real harm done," Tulip said.

Rose pouted. "It makes me feel bad."

"*Jah.* I know what you mean. Does Mark know you like Jacob?"

"I think he does and that's why he invited me to dinner."

"You and Mark were over before you even began," Tulip said.

"Pretend over, and pretend began. Don't forget that," Rose pointed out.

"Mark must be upset about you liking his cousin."

"*Nee.* Well, a little bit at first, but he invited me to dinner tomorrow night to see him. He knows I'm just a friend and that's all we'll ever be."

"How old is Jacob?"

"I don't know anything about him except that he's here to learn how to make buggies with his *onkel.* The rest doesn't matter. I'll find out all I can tomorrow night if *Mamm* and *Dat* let me go. I'll go downstairs now and hope *Mamm's* told him about it."

Before Rose made a move, a gentle knock sounded on her bedroom door. "Rose, your *vadder* and I would like to speak with you now."

Rose looked at Tulip for emotional and moral support. The next few minutes would determine if she was going to that dinner or not. "Okay. I'm coming," she called back.

"I hope things go well," Tulip whispered.

Rose whispered back, "*Denke.* Stay here and I'll tell you about it when I come back. I'm either going to be very happy or upset."

"I'll wait. If *Mamm's* sort of said you can go, you've got a good chance."

Rose left Tulip and went downstairs to face what her parents had decided.

From the looks on both their faces, she felt she was in trouble.

Her mother began, as soon as Rose sat in front of them on the opposite couch, "I told your *vadder* that you and Mark are over and you're not interested in him any longer."

"That's right."

"So you were seeing him, and now you're not?" her mother asked.

"*Jah*, that's right."

"And exactly how long were you and he—"

"Rose doesn't have to tell us all the small details," her father said.

"I was just asking because it seems odd. She never mentioned a thing about him until the other day, and as soon as I asked him to come to dinner, she's not dating him anymore."

"Anyway, he won't be coming over for dinner tomorrow night because that would be awkward," Rose said. "He said he hoped you both don't mind and—"

"He can still come." Her mother frowned. "You're still friends, and I invited him."

"*Mamm*, do you forget I mentioned that I'm going to Mark's house for dinner because his cousin is visiting?"

"A man or a woman?" her father asked.

Before Rose could answer, her mother said, "It's Jacob Schumacher?"

"*Jah*, I guess that's his last name. His first name is Jacob and he's staying at Mark's *haus*. Do you know him, *Dat*?"

"I do."

Her mother turned toward Rose's father. "Well, what do you think of him?"

"I only met him today at the bishop's *haus*. He seems a nice young man."

Her mother wasn't finished. "And what community does he come from?"

"He comes from Oakes County," Rose's father said.

"Why did Mark ask you to dinner, Rose?"

"Because I met Jacob at the markets today. Mark thought it would be a good idea if we had dinner at his place. I don't know; maybe Jacob wants to meet people while he's here."

"*Nee*," her mother spat out the word.

"*Mamm*, what's the matter?"

"What you're saying isn't adding up. Something's not right here."

"Nancy, I can't think of a reason Rose shouldn't have dinner at Mark's *haus*. We know the family well. What harm could it do?"

"I didn't say it would do harm. I just don't think we're hearing the full story. That's why I wanted to talk with you in front of your *vadder*, Rose, because you might be more inclined to tell him what's really going on in your life."

"You know how young people can be, Nancy."

Nancy crossed her arms over her chest and Rose's father whispered, "We don't need to hear the whole story, Nancy."

Rose remained stony-faced, as though she hadn't heard his whispered words. She was grateful to her father for allowing her some space.

"Did you want to say anything else to Rose?" her father asked her mother.

Her mother shook her head. "Well, if you're happy with her explanation, we'll leave it at that."

"Well, *Dat*?" Rose asked.

"I think everything's been said. We trust you to make the right decision here, Rose, and not do anything behind our backs. The worst thing parents can face is their child getting into trouble or getting themselves into harm's way."

"Okay, but it's just dinner, *Dat*, and it's at the Schumachers.'"

"Your *vadder* is talking about the other thing where you're not telling us the full story. You didn't have a boyfriend, the next day you do, and then the next day it's all over, and you've got your heart set on someone else. It doesn't add up."

Rose would've preferred if her mother hadn't said all those things in front of her father. Especially the thing about having her heart set on another man. "I'm not doing anything wrong, I'm safe, and I'm not putting myself in harm's way. Mark and I have ended things and we're still friends. We handled things like adults."

"That's very good to hear," her father said.

"Are you happy with what she's just said, Hezekiah?"

He turned to his wife. "I am, are you?"

"Not totally, but we'll leave it at that for now."

Rose leaped to her feet. "Can I go now?"

"*Jah*, you can go," her father said.

"And I can go to Mark's for dinner tomorrow, *jah*?"

"Okay," her mother said.

"Denke, Mamm and *Dat."* She gave them both a quick kiss on the cheek and then wasted no time hurrying up the stairs. When she was back in her room, she threw herself onto her bed, missing Tulip by inches.

"What happened?" Tulip asked as she got up off the bed to shut the door.

When she sat back on the bed, Rose sighed. "Weren't you listening in?"

"I tried to, but I couldn't hear everything."

"Mamm doesn't believe that Mark and I were in a relationship and now she thinks something is odd about me liking Jacob. She should be happy since she's trying to get me married off."

"Now both *Mamm* and *Dat* know you like Jacob?"

"I guess they do."

"That seems strange."

"I know, but I can't do anything about it now." Rose exhaled deeply.

"It's just that they might say something to someone. Parents have a habit of doing things like that and embarrassing their *kinner.*"

Rose giggled. "That's true, but I don't think it matters. I think that Jacob likes me just as much as I like him. I've got that feeling. We have a deep connection."

"I wish I had someone like that. Someone to love and admire."

"You will. I had no one and now I've got Jacob." Rose giggled. "I haven't really got him yet, but I've got him to think about."

"To daydream about," said Tulip.

"Jah."

Chapter Eight

Greater love hath no man than this, that a man lay down his life for his friends.

John 15:13

Rose woke early the next morning. She had to make herself look the best she could because she wouldn't have time to change before going to Mark's house later that night for dinner.

She pulled on her dressing gown to shield herself from the chilly morning air, and when she took up her hairbrush, she placed it in her lap. Each night she carefully braided her hair, so it wouldn't tangle during the night while she slept. She untied her hair and it fell in waves well below her waist. Her hair had never been cut. After she'd brushed out her hair with one hundred long smooth strokes, she re-braided it and pinned it flat against her head in order for it to fit under her white starched prayer *kapp*.

Rose turned her attention to her home-sewn dresses made with the treadle-machine. She had five dresses each a different color. The pale yellow dress would give her skin a little more depth, she decided. She'd always felt good in yellow for some reason. She wondered which one Jacob would like. Maybe he'd prefer her in the green dress? Her eyes flickered over the grape-colored one; then she decided to save that one to wear at the Sunday meeting. The dark green one was quickly discarded as that was a shade that many of the older ladies wore. She wanted to look young and vibrant, so she went back to her first choice of the yellow dress.

After she had pulled her dress on, she placed her apron over the top, expertly tying the strings behind her back. When she was fully dressed, she sat and looked out the window at the horizon. The sun was barely evident behind the distant hills, giving the sky around them a warm and happy glow.

The moon had set, its light all but faded, while one lone star twinkled brightly toward the west against the remaining backdrop of navy blue.

It was rare that Rose was awake so early and she reminded herself she should enjoy that hour more often. It was so beautiful to watch the night fade as it greeted the morning. It was a display of God's beauty.

Her wonder was interrupted when she heard a gentle tap on her door. She knew it couldn't have been her sisters awake so early because they never knocked. Instead, they'd just walk right in. It had to be her father.

She leaped off her bed and opened her door. "Morning, *Dat*," she said when she saw his smiling face.

"I thought I heard you awake."

"*Jah*, it's going to be a busy day because I'm going from work to Mark's *haus*."

"I know. I remember."

"It must be early if you haven't left for work yet."

"I'm just going down to eat. Your *mudder* has got my breakfast ready. I just wanted to tell you to be careful. I know your *Mamm's* got it into her mind that you should marry someone and marry him fast. That's just how she is. She thinks of something and then she wants it done immediately." He chuckled quietly and had softness in his eyes the way he always did when he talked about his wife. "I'm not going against what she says. I'm just saying to be cautious."

Rose tilted her head to the side. They kept telling her to be cautious as though she were a child. "About what?"

"The decisions you make now, while you're young, can affect the rest of your life." There was a silent moment between them. "Do you know what I mean?"

"*Nee*, not really."

"Picture this then: You get into a boat and you're on a journey. You pull up anchor and set your sail in a certain direction, and the current pulls you in that same direction faster and faster. Pretty soon you're a long way from where you started, and the problem is there's just no way to get back. Meaning you can't start over once you've set sail."

It sounded quite a frightening story the way he told it. "Doesn't the current go the other way?"

"In my story, the current is time, and it only goes in the one direction, and there's no way to go back and start over. Once you set the direction of the sails, that's it. Be careful which way you set them because you might fall asleep and when you wake, you'll find that you want to be over there and you're over here, with no way to get where you want to be."

She stared at her father's worried face and the deep lines in his forehead, knowing he didn't know a thing at all about boats. She tried to interpret what he just said. "So be careful what direction I go in, and don't fall asleep?"

"You've got it." He put his hand gently on her shoulder and stared into her face. "Determine what direction you want to go and, if it turns out that that direction doesn't suit, adjust the sails quickly before you go too far in that other direction."

"The bad direction?"

He nodded. "But consider all directions carefully. The wrong direction might look like the right one when it isn't."

"Got it."

He stepped back and smiled. "Your *mudder* will be wondering where I am."

"*Denke, Dat.* I won't be late home tonight."

"Shall I come and collect you from the Schumachers'?"

"*Nee,* I'm sure Mark or his cousin will give me a ride home." Rose couldn't help the tiny smile that tugged at the corners of her lips. It would be wonderful and romantic if Jacob drove her home in the darkness under the starlit sky.

Her father walked away and Rose closed her door. She knew the translation of her father's boat talk; it was he telling her to be careful whom she married. If she chose the wrong man, she had to change her mind before she married him, otherwise, it would be too late. There was no divorce in their Amish community, and she'd seen a few unhappy marriages. In those cases, the couples had chosen to live separately. It seemed a miserable existence and she'd listen to her father's caution.

She gave a little chuckle thinking how funny her father was with his scenarios. Why couldn't he just speak his mind and talk about men and marriage? Rose went back to the window and sat back down. The sun had just peeped over the horizon giving a glow of light to the distant hills.

She closed her eyes and prayed that Jacob would realize that she was the woman for him. Hopefully, he felt the same attraction as she.

When Rose walked into the farmers market, she saw Mark talking to someone at the entrance. She walked right on past without saying a word.

"Hey," he called out to her.

She turned around to look at him.

He said goodbye to the person he'd been talking with and hurried to her. "Are we on, or are we off?"

"In our relationship? Or dinner tonight?"

"I meant our relationship." They continued walking to their stalls.

"We're off," Rose said bluntly.

He rubbed his chin. "Oh, that's too bad."

She frowned at him. Yesterday he was upset with her about it, saying it would be too hard to pretend they were a couple.

He continued, "You can still make it for dinner tonight, can't you?"

"*Jah*, I can, if that's still alright. Jacob will be there, won't he?"

Mark nodded while they continued to walk inside the market. "Jacob will be there."

"Okay."

"You look nice today, Rosie. That color really suits you. It brings out the golden flecks in your eyes."

She laughed. "I don't have golden flecks in my eyes. My eyes are just green."

"You do. You have tiny flakes of gold surrounding

your pupils. And the rest of your eyes are as green as precious emeralds."

She smiled because she recalled those same golden flecks in Jacob's brown eyes, which would mean their children would quite possibly have the golden flecks too.

"What did your folks say about dinner, and me not coming? Are they okay with that? I hope they weren't too sad that I'm not going to be there."

"I told them we were no longer together, and that you had your cousin visiting, so you invited me over. *Dat* said that he met Jacob at the bishop's *haus* yesterday."

"Oh, I didn't know that, but Jacob mentioned he was visiting a few people when he left here."

"I think *Mamm* thinks I'm a bit odd now."

"Her too?"

Rose giggled and slapped him on the shoulder. "Stop it."

"Why does she think you're odd? For ending things with me? If so, I totally understand that, and now I know for sure she's a wise woman."

"*Nee.* She thinks I'm odd because I told her we were a secret, and then suddenly I had to take it back and tell them we were no longer together. Not only that, I'm going to dinner at your *haus.*"

"That's not odd; that happens all the time."

"Not with me it doesn't," Rose said just as she reached her stall.

"Well, don't be too upset about us breaking up. We can still be friends." He sniggered.

"That's another thing my folks thought odd and strange—me going to your place for dinner after we're no longer together. Well, *Mamm* did more so than *Dat.* I explained to them that we're still friends and that your cousin would be there."

He shook his head. "You do get yourself into some awkward situations, Rosie."

"*Nee*, I don't! This was the first awkward thing that's happened, and don't forget it was your suggestion in the first place."

He chuckled. "And you're never going to let me live that down, are you?"

She shook her head. "Never!"

Rose kept busy by arranging the flowers. She loved working with them—she was happiest when flowers and their fragrance surrounded her. Despite her name being Rose, her favorite flowers were daisies. They were such happy flowers and filled her heart with joy, as she imagined their central section as smiling faces. Daisies also reminded her of when she was young when she'd sit in the fields on lazy summer days, making daisy chains with Tulip. The twins were babies back then. Her mother would spread out a large blanket, and Tulip and she would sit for hours after their mother had shown them how to make the flowers intersect one another to create the daisy chains.

For the remainder of the day, Rose purposefully tried not to think of Jacob and the wonderful life they'd have together. She didn't want to let her mind run away with her until she knew for sure that Jacob felt the same. Instead of daydreaming about Jacob, she concentrated on work. Every now and again, she got nervous pangs in her stomach about seeing him again. Her entire future hinged on this dinner. She'd surely find out if Jacob truly liked her.

Chapter Nine

He that loveth not knoweth not God; for God is love.
1 John 4:8

The workday had been a struggle where Rose had to purposefully push her nerves aside and forget about the dinner she'd be going to that evening. Every time she thought about seeing Jacob again, she started to worry that he hadn't felt the same attraction, or if he had, he might change his mind over dinner.

At the end of the day, Mr. Walker himself collected the flowers and the takings, instead of one of his older sons. Rose waited for Mark to finish up serving the last of his customers.

"Are you ready now?" Rose asked when the customers walked away. She tried hard to keep the impatience from her voice.

"*Jah*, unless I get some more customers. That's why we're here, Rosie, to make money, remember?"

"I know, but it's after our normal closing time."

"Is it?" He glanced at the large clock that hung over the middle of the aisle. "So it is."

He was deliberately going slow just to annoy her, she

was certain. "I'll help you pack." All the cheese had to be locked down in the fridges overnight.

"No need. I do it by myself all the time."

"I insist," Rose said.

Minutes later, Rose walked with Mark to his buggy.

Before she got in, he said, "It's only about twenty minutes to my *haus*. I hope you can control yourself with me for that long—sitting so close to me in this luxurious buggy of mine."

Rose pulled a face at the ancient buggy that was barely road-worthy. "I could always sit in the back if you're that worried."

He laughed. "No need for that. I'm sure I can trust you." They headed out of the lot, where the horse and buggy had been for the day, and moved onto the road.

"I hope your parents weren't too upset when they learned we weren't together anymore."

Rose played along. "They were absolutely devastated. It will take them some time to recover. Maybe even years."

Mark chuckled. "I would imagine it would. They can see I am a reliable hardworking man and what more could they want in a husband for you?"

"Let's see now. One who is kind, caring and unselfish?"

He glanced over at her taking his eyes from the road for one second. "I'm all those things."

"I know you are," she said hoping she hadn't gone too far with her teasing. The last thing she wanted to do was offend him.

"Well then, your search is over."

Even though Rose didn't want to hurt his feelings, neither did she want him getting in the way when she was trying to talk to Jacob over dinner. "You will make someone happy one day, Mark."

"*Jah*, I believe I will."

Rose kept the conversation away from Jacob even though she was anxious to learn all she could about him.

"Here we are," Mark said when they finally pulled up beside his family home. "I'll take you in, and then I'll need to come back out and tend to the horse."

"You don't need to come in with me. I can go in by myself."

"Are you sure?"

"Of course I am." She got down from the buggy, looking all around to see if she could see Jacob, but he was nowhere in sight. He had to be inside the house. "*Denke*, Mark," she called over her shoulder as she walked to the house.

"No problem," she heard him call back.

She knocked on the door and Mark's mother opened it. Mark was the second youngest child of eleven children, all of who had left home except for Mark and his younger brother, Matthew.

"Rose, how lovely to see you." With both hands, she reached out and clasped Rose's forearm. "Come inside. I'm always telling Mark to invite you for dinner. I don't know what took both of you so long."

"*Denke*. That's nice of you." Rose had struggled to find words. She hadn't expected such a friendly response. It was as though Mark's mother thought there was something between her and Mark. Could Mark have made out that there was? It *was* something he'd do.

"We've got a visitor, Mark's cousin from Oakes County."

"*Jah*, I've met Jacob. He stopped by the market stall yesterday."

Mark's mother ignored what she said, and continued to pull her into the living room where Jacob sat with Mr. Schumacher, Mark's father.

Both men stood when they entered the room. "Jacob, this is a good friend of Mark's, Rose."

Jacob nodded. "*Jah*, we've met before, just yesterday."

"Hello, Rose," Mr. Schumacher said.

"Hello, Mr. Schumacher," Rose answered doing her best to look at the older man when all she wanted to do was fix her eyes onto Jacob.

They all stood there staring at Rose, and she licked her lips wondering what she should do. She looked back at Mrs. Schumacher. "Would you like some help with anything in the kitchen?" Rose wanted to speak to Jacob alone, but didn't want to speak to him with Mr. Schumacher listening.

"*Nee*, you're our guest. Sit down and tell us what you've been doing lately. I never get a chance to speak to you at the meetings."

Mrs. Schumacher guided Rose to the couch, and Rose sat down next to Jacob.

When they were all seated, Rose looked around at the three sets of eyes on her. She felt like she was back in school where she had to stand and speak in front of the whole class. Her stomach clenched now, as it had then, and she felt she would be sick.

Rose took a deep breath to steady her nerves before she spoke. "I haven't been doing anything much. Just going to work."

"Rose works at the Walkers' flower stall at the farmers market," Mark's father explained to Jacob.

Jacob smiled. "I know, right next to Mark's stall. I saw Mark there yesterday and I met Rose at the same time."

Again, Rose felt nervous as the three of them stared at her again. "That's all I've got to say." It was a lame response, but it was either that or silence.

"How many brothers and sisters do you have?" Jacob asked.

"I have two older brothers and three younger sisters."

"The younger two girls are twins," Mrs. Schumacher explained to Jacob.

Jacob smiled as he told Rose, "My two older brothers are twins and they married twin sisters."

"That is unusual, but I think I've heard of twins marrying twins before. I've never personally known anybody who did." Rose looked at Mark's parents hoping they'd both leave the room so she could be alone with Jacob. Jacob was looking at her as though he were thinking the very same thing. At least, that's what Rose hoped was going on in his mind.

"How long are you here for, Jacob?" she asked, even though she knew the answer from the day before.

"I don't know exactly. I'm here for a few weeks, anyway, to learn about the buggy making from Harry. There's a permanent job on offer, but I'm not certain whether to take it or not. My uncle said to try it for a few weeks to see what I think so that's what I'm doing."

Rose was delighted to hear about the job offer. Harry was the local buggy maker and people came from far and wide to buy their buggies from him. Rose was sure Harry had around six men working for him.

"And have you done buggy making before?" she asked Jacob.

"Never, that's why I'm trying it." He laughed and Rose felt a little silly for asking a dumb question. It was just nerves. He continued, "It's something I've always thought about doing as a trade. I'm an upholsterer already, so I know how to do that side of things."

"*Jah*, which would come in handy, I'd imagine."

At that moment, Mark walked in and sat down with them.

His mother turned to look at him. "Mark, how was your day?"

"It was a fairly good day. We had above average takings."

"*Gut!*" his father said.

Chapter Ten

Better are the wounds of a friend, than the deceitful kisses of an enemy.

Proverbs 27:6

"I don't know how you do it, working at that stall all day," Jacob said to Mark.

"The market stall provides a good income for the whole family," Mr. Schumacher explained before Mark responded again.

"I quite enjoy it. I like meeting new people, and taking care of the same customers who come back week after week. I'm good friends with many of them now."

Mrs. Schumacher said, "Mark is a people person. He's always been outgoing and friendly, even when he was a little *bu.*"

Rose quietly agreed. Everyone liked Mark.

Jacob grimaced and looked at Mark. "Doesn't it get smelly working around goat cheese?" He waved his hand in front of his screwed-up nose.

Frowning at Jacob's rudeness, Mark said, "*Nee!* Anyway, we sell nearly everything to do with goats. We have goats' milk soap, yoghurt, and milk; not just cheese."

"*Jah*, you'll need that soap to get the goats' smell off." Jacob laughed but no one joined him.

"It's no more smelly work than, say, buggy making," Mark replied now looking either serious or annoyed at his cousin.

"That's not smelly at all." Jacob glared at Mark.

Sensing the mounting tension in the air, Rose said, "I have the smelliest job of all."

Everyone looked at Rose and laughed.

"I think the word you're looking for, Rose, is 'fragrant,'" Mr. Schumacher said.

"*Jah*, that sounds much better," Rose commented.

"Dinner smells delicious, Aunt Sally," Jacob said to Mrs. Schumacher.

"I hope you like it, it's—"

"Goat stew?" Jacob asked.

Mr. Schumacher laughed, while Mark scowled at him.

"I'm sorry, Mark, I was just trying to be funny," Jacob said. "Your *vadder* thought it was funny."

"Our goats are for milking, not eating," Mark said.

Jacob continued, "Surely you eat the older ones—"

"*Nee*, don't talk about that please." Rose covered her ears.

"It's lamb stew, a recipe I got from your *onkel's* dear old *mudder*, your *Grossmammi* Schumacher, and Mark's." She looked at Rose. "She's gone to be with *Gott* now."

"I'm pretty sure I remember her," Rose said.

"It's Mark's favorite food," Mrs. Schumacher said smiling at her son.

Rose kept talking, hoping Jacob wouldn't say anything else to upset Mark. "I can't wait to try it."

"Well you can, in about five minutes as soon as Matthew gets home."

"Are you sure you don't need any help?" Rose asked.

"Maybe we could leave the men alone for a few minutes. Will you help me in the kitchen, Rose?"

Rose stood and followed Mark's mother into the kitchen while thinking that it might have been better if Mark had arranged some sort of outing with just a few young people including her and Jacob. It was awkward having a family dinner at Mark's house with Mr. and Mrs. Schumacher listening to everything that was said.

Halfway through dinner, Rose wished she had invited Tulip along after all. Rose wasn't much of a talker and it had been difficult to keep the conversation flowing as well as stopping the tension between Mark and Jacob. Matthew had sat there and barely said a word.

It was after dessert that Mark's younger brother excused himself and Mr. and Mrs. Schumacher left the other three young people alone in the kitchen to talk.

"Would you like coffee, Rosie?" Mark asked.

"*Jah*, I would. Do you want me to get it?"

"*Nee*, I can do it. What about you, Jacob?"

"*Jah*, I wouldn't mind one."

Mark went to the far end of the kitchen and put the pot on the stove to boil.

"Do you know what you're doing, Mark?" Rose asked with a giggle.

"Don't you worry about me, Rosie."

"He knows what he's doing in the kitchen. He'll make someone a good *fraa* one day." Jacob laughed hard at his own joke.

Rose smiled even though she didn't find it very funny, and Mark ignored him as he got the cups ready for the coffee.

Jacob turned his attention back to Rose. "So, is it Rose, or Rosie?"

"It's Rose, but Mark likes to call me Rosie for some reason."

"I'll call you Rose. I like the name Rose."

"Okay." It didn't matter what he called her. She liked the deep rich tones of his voice.

"Rose, we've got the meeting on Sunday morning. What are you doing after that?" Jacob asked.

"Nothing that I know of."

Jacob leaned closer and said quietly, "How about we do something together?"

The metal coffee container in Mark's hands slipped from his grasp and clanged heavily on the floor, scattering the ground coffee everywhere. The container bounced across the room and stopped just near the doorway.

Rose jumped up to help Mark clean up the mess while Jacob laughed.

"Thanks, Rosie," Mark said. "It looks like we won't be having coffee after all. How about some hot tea instead?"

"Tea will be fine. You go ahead and make the tea and I'll clean this up," Rose said. "Just tell me where the broom and the dustpan are."

"Through that door."

Jacob hadn't moved from his spot at the kitchen table. "I was looking forward to coffee."

"You still can have it. I'll scrape some off the floor for you," Mark said.

Jacob shook his head. "I'll take a pass on that one."

Rose sat on one side of the table sipping hot tea, while looking at both Jacob and Mark. It was like being between two roosters that wanted to fight each other. Jacob had attempted to ask her out, but she didn't know how to get the conversation back to where it had been before Mark's coffee-spilling incident.

Perhaps if she jogged Jacob's memory a little he'd ask her again, or would that appear too desperate? No, she would have to wait until Jacob mentioned something of his own accord.

"So, you have twins in your *familye*?" Jacob asked her.

"That's right. Daisy and Lily. They're younger than I am."

"I've got two older brothers who are twins."

Rose nodded politely, wondering why he didn't remember that they'd already talked about that before dinner. "*Jah*, I think I heard something along those lines."

Jacob turned to his cousin. "Mark, why don't you be a good son and see if your parents would like some hot tea?"

It was a large hint for Mark to leave them alone in the kitchen and Rose hoped he'd take it.

"*Nee*, they wouldn't. *Denke* for your concern. They never have hot tea after dinner. Sometimes they have coffee, but now they won't be having that."

Jacob turned back to look at Rose and from the way he looked at her, she knew that if Mark had not been there he would've asked her out. All hope wasn't lost. Maybe at the meeting on Sunday he would ask her out again.

When the time came for her to go home, both Mark and Jacob insisted on driving her. It was Mark's buggy so he won the argument, but Jacob had insisted on going along for the ride.

"There's no reason why it won't."

"Shall we have a cup of hot tea?"

Rose shook her head. "*Nee.* I had an early start this morning. I'll go to bed."

"And think about Jacob?"

"It's been hard not to think about him. I can't keep him out of my mind. I only hope that he feels the same."

"He does. I'm sure of it."

"I hope so."

Rose switched off the main overhead gaslight and carried a small lantern up the stairs to light their way. Then each girl went to her own room.

After she'd pushed her bedroom door open with her foot, Rose placed the lantern on her dresser and got ready for bed. She hoped that everything would turn out as she planned.

Once she was between the sheets, she imagined what it might be like to be married to Jacob and have children with him. Just like the twins often said, she too would like three sets of twins so there would only be three childbirths. The children would all have the golden flecks in their eyes, as Jacob and she shared that in common. Would Jacob be happy to stay on in this small community? Or would he go home in a few weeks? If he wanted to go back home, Rose would go with him if he asked her.

Once she was married with her own home, everyone would stop looking over her shoulder and trying to run her life. She'd be happy and independent. Rose drifted sweetly off to sleep while imagining she was married to Jacob, living in a clean tidy house with their three adorable sets of twins. Life would be perfect.

When they reached the house, Jacob looked out at it. "So this is where you live, Rose?"

"It is."

"It's quite big," Jacob said. "It looks so from the outside."

"*Jah,* none of us has ever had to share a bedroom even when the boys lived at home. There was a bedroom for each of us. Now *Mamm* has a sewing room and *Dat* uses one as an office since the boys are married and gone."

Through the windows she could see warm lights coming from both the kitchen and the dining rooms. Without walking inside, Rose knew that Tulip had been waiting up for her, wanting to hear what happened and she couldn't wait to tell her everything.

"*Denke* for driving me home, Mark."

"*Denke* for coming to dinner."

"It was good to get to know you better, Rose. I'm sure I'll see a lot more of you soon," Jacob said. "And I would've driven you home if my cousin hadn't insisted on coming with us."

"I've driven Rose home. You've come with me," Mark pointed out to Jacob.

"*Denke.*" Rose gave him a nod.

When Rose got down from the buggy, she headed into the house and the moment she opened the door, she turned and gave a little wave. It was too dark to see if the two men were looking at her as Mark's horse *clip-clopped* back down the driveway.

Rose closed the door behind her and leaned against it. She knew Mark liked her, but now there was Jacob, whom she hoped liked her. There had been tension between Jacob and Mark the whole night. Next time she'd have to get Jacob away by himself somewhere away from Mark. If only Mark hadn't spilled that coffee right when he had. It had been such an awkward night. No wonder Matthew excused himself and went to bed early. He probably sensed the tension too.

"How was it?"

On hearing Tulip's voice, Rose looked up to see her sister rushing down the stairs toward her. Rose took off her shawl and hung it on the wooden peg by the door.

"Quickly tell me, or I'll simply burst."

Rose giggled and carefully looked around to ensure they were alone. "Let's sit by the fireplace where it's warm."

The two girls sat by the fire, which had nearly burned to nothing.

"I'm sure he likes me," Rose whispered.

"That's so great. How do you know?"

"I can tell. He tried to ask me out, but Mark got in the way."

"Oh, that's too bad. What does he look like?"

"I've already told you that."

"Tell me again. I have no boyfriend. I have to live through you and let your excitement be my excitement."

"He's not my boyfriend. Not yet anyway."

Both girls giggled and then Rose told Tulip about the awkward evening.

"Rose, he was just about to ask you out. Do you think Mark dropped that coffee tin deliberately?"

"He wouldn't have done that. At least, I don't think so. He was the one who invited me there in the first place."

"*Jah*, but it's no secret he likes you; he always has."

"I just wish that I could've been alone with Jacob and gotten to know him better."

"At least you found out a lot, and the reason he's here."

"The worst thing was that he mentioned going somewhere together after the meeting tomorrow."

"That's fantastic!"

Rose shook her head. "I don't know."

"Why is that bad?"

"Because he was interrupted when he was talking. I never got a chance to say yes and he never asked again."

"So you're not going anywhere with him tomorrow afternoon?"

"I don't know."

"It seems complicated. Tell me again what happened?"

"Haven't you been listening?"

"*Jah*, but I'm tired. Tell me again."

"That was when Mark had the accident with the coffee. I need you to do me a huge favor on Sunday."

Tulip leaned forward. "What is it?"

"I'll introduce you to Jacob and I want you to get friendly with him and then maybe mention that the four of us might go somewhere together."

"The four of us? Meaning you, me, him, and Mark?"

"Exactly! That way, I'll get to spend time with him and it won't look like I've asked him."

Tulip pouted. "*Nee*, it won't look like you've asked him because I would've asked him. That's not what I'd normally do."

"Well, will you do it? Do it for me?" Rose put h[er] hands together and pouted trying to make her sister sorry for her.

Tulip smiled. "Okay. I'll do it if you want me [to,] only if you'll do the same for me one day, or som[ething] similar if I need you to."

Rose nodded. "*Jah*. We have a deal. *Gut!* W[hen we're] all together, just the four of us, you keep M[ark busy] and right out of the way so I can have time [with Jacob.]"

Tulip giggled. "I hope that will work."

Chapter Eleven

For we are saved by hope: but hope that is seen is not hope: for what a man seeth, why doth he yet hope for?

Romans 8:24

Rose was up early on Sunday morning, making sure she looked her best for Jacob. Still, she was the last one down to the kitchen.

"Quick! You better hurry," Tulip said as she rinsed out a few dishes at the sink.

"I'm ready."

"You haven't eaten yet," her mother said.

"I'm not hungry."

"You'll need something in your stomach," her mother protested. She was always trying to force as much food into her children as she could.

Rose reached forward and grabbed an apple from the bowl in the center of the table. "I'll have one of these," she said before she bit into it.

"At least that's something, I suppose," her mother said.

"I'll eat after the meeting. There's always so much food."

"Don't look too hungry when you eat. I don't want people to think we aren't feeding you enough or that you wait for after the meetings to have a decent feed."

"No one's going to think that. Everyone knows we get fed."

"You're thin because you don't eat enough, and there's nothing natural about that. I don't think men like women who are too skinny. You should keep that in mind. Men like women to have meat on their bones. And if you had more padding you wouldn't look so tall. Men like women to be shorter than them."

"Jah, Mamm." Rose wondered how her mother knew so much about what men liked, since *Mamm* had married young, and *Dat* had been her only boyfriend.

Her mother looked out the window. "Quick, your *vadder* has the buggy hitched. Come on, all of you. Now!"

Rose wore her grape-colored dress in the hopes that Jacob would like it. She got compliments when she wore it from girls her age.

They arrived at the Fullers' *haus* where the fortnightly Sunday meeting was being held. The twins hurried off to meet their friends while Tulip and Rose walked more slowly behind them.

"Don't forget what I said to do," Rose said.

"I remember. You'll introduce me to Jacob, then I get to talking to him and suggest the four of us go somewhere, right?"

"That's right."

"Got it. Do you think this will work?"

"I'm hoping so."

"You look pretty today, Rose. What have you done to yourself?"

"It's the fresh bloom of love."

Tulip giggled. "Well, if you could bottle that, we could sell it at the markets."

The two girls giggled again. Rose caught sight of Jacob heading into the house, and caught Tulip's arm. "That's him."

Tulip stood on her tiptoes. "I can't see anyone."

"That's because he's just now gone into the *haus*."

"Let's sit down at the back, and then you can point him out to me."

"Good idea, but you'll know him when you see him. He'll probably be the only stranger in the meeting."

"I like sitting at the back anyway, then I can watch everyone."

As soon as Rose walked into the house, Jacob was right there smiling at her. She smiled back as she walked past him with Tulip beside her.

"Was that him?" Tulip whispered.

"*Jah*. What do you think?"

"He looks very nice. Isn't he too old for you?"

"*Nee*, of course not."

They slid into the back row.

"I've always seen you, in my mind, with someone more like Mark," Tulip said.

Rose's jaw fell open. "Don't be ridiculous! Mark is just a friend. I wouldn't marry a friend!"

"It'd be better than marrying an enemy."

Rose whispered back, "I'm not going to do either. The person I'm going to marry is sitting right there in the second row from the front."

"That's where Mark's sitting."

"That's also where Jacob's sitting and he's the one I'm going to marry. Don't be annoying."

"I'm just sayin' the truth of what I feel."

"It's what I feel that's important because it's my life."

"Okay."

Rose whispered, "Don't start getting to be like *Mamm.*"

Tulip dug her sister in the ribs. "I'm not like *Mamm.*"

"Well don't speak like her."

Tulip nodded. "I'll help you in any way that I can."

Rose looked at her sister and gave her a big smile. *"Denke."*

The girls' father stood and opened the meeting in prayer, and then Joseph Oleff sang a song in High German. When Joseph was finished, the bishop stood and began his sermon.

Rose always liked to hear what the bishop had to say. He usually told stories about real life situations, and then drew similarities from the stories in the Bible.

Rose's mother was one of the women who got up during the last ten minutes of the service to set out the food. There was always a big meal served after the meeting, and the other ladies yielded to *Mamm* as the organizer. Since Sunday was a day of rest, no one worked except to do the jobs that were necessities, such as feeding animals and the like, and the food for Sunday's meals was prepared the day before.

Chapter Twelve

And now abideth faith, hope, charity, these three;
but the greatest of these is charity.

1 Corinthians 13:13

On Sunday, Rose was clever enough to arrange things so that the twins were helping their mother with the food after the meeting. And that left Rose and Tulip free to socialize, and talk with Jacob.

After the meeting had come to an end, people had walked out of the house into the yard where the food and refreshment tables were.

Rose whispered to Tulip, "Let's go up to the drinks table and get a soda. And then, we'll just wait there and hope Jacob comes over."

The two girls got a soda each and stayed back from the table while they talked to one another. It wasn't long before Jacob approached them and Rose introduced Jacob to Tulip.

"How long are you staying here for, Jacob?" asked Tulip.

"I'll be here for quite a few weeks. I'm staying with Mark's *familye*."

"Do you know many people here in the community?" Tulip asked.

"*Nee*, I don't."

Rose stared at Tulip. This was the perfect time for her to say what they'd planned.

"The four of us should do something some time. The three of us and Mark."

"What a good idea," Rose commented as though she was hearing it for the first time.

"Okay, what do you think we should do?" Jacob asked with a smile.

Tulip answered, "I'm not sure. We could go on a picnic or something."

"Why don't we do it this afternoon?" Jacob asked, now turning to Rose. "Are you free later today, Rose?"

"*Jah*, I am. I guess we could do that." While she was talking, she saw Mark walking to them.

Tulip saw him too. "Mark, we're planning on doing something this afternoon. Can you join us?"

Rose couldn't help smiling as she listened and watched her brilliant plan unfold.

"Unless you had some other plans, Mark?" Jacob asked.

"Why don't we have a picnic?" Mark asked the girls, ignoring Jacob.

"A picnic sounds like a good idea," Tulip said. "That's what we were just talking about. I think it was my idea first."

Mark laughed and was just about to say something when Jacob interrupted him.

"How about we collect you girls at, say, around two o'clock this afternoon?" Jacob asked.

Tulip and Rose nodded.

"That suits us," Rose said.

"You don't want to stay on for the singing?" Mark asked.

"You can stay," Jacob said. "If I can borrow your buggy, I'll go on a picnic with the girls by myself."

"*Nee*, you won't. I'll go too. We'll collect you girls at two."

"We'll be ready," Tulip said. "So shall we bring the food?"

"We can bring the drink and the dessert if you girls can make some sandwiches," Mark suggested.

"We can do that," Rose said.

"Good. We'll see you at two."

Rose knew she'd have to do some careful negotiations with her parents. Of a Sunday, Rose normally took her parents home and then went back for the young people's singing where she would drive the twins and Tulip back home.

Rose found her father and considered he'd be the easiest to talk with first. "*Dat*, Tulip and I would like to go on a picnic with Mark and Jacob this afternoon at two. Do you mind if you collect the twins from the singing just this once?"

He rubbed his graying beard. "Have you asked your *mudder*?"

"*Nee*, I'm asking you first. Please don't say that I can if it's all right with her."

One dark eyebrow raised just slightly. "How did you know I was going to say that?"

Rose grunted. "Really?"

His mouth turned upward at the corners. "That's what I was going to say. I don't think she'll mind." He nodded his head. "There she is. Ask her."

She glanced where he'd pointed his head and saw her,

and then said to her father, "So, if it's okay with her, I can go? You don't have a problem with it?"

"*Nee.* If it's okay with *Mamm*, it's okay with me. Just don't be late home."

"I don't know what time we'll be back. What if we want to go to dinner somewhere afterward?"

"Don't be later than eight thirty."

"Okay. I won't. I mean, we won't. Tulip's coming too."

"Very good."

Rose hurried over to her mother. To her surprise, her mother didn't seem to mind in the least. Either that, or she wanted to appear trusting of her daughter to those who'd overheard Rose's request.

Everything was falling neatly into place. Rose hurried to tell Tulip the good news.

By the time Rose, Tulip, and their parents got home, the girls only had an hour before Mark and Jacob were due to collect them. Rose sat on her bed while Tulip tried to calm her.

"Why have you got so nervous all of the sudden?"

"Because I really like him."

"He likes you too or he wouldn't have agreed to go on the picnic."

Rose rubbed her forehead. "Do you think so?"

"*Jah*, I know it. Now, are you going to stay in that dress?"

Rose looked down. "Do you think I should change it? I don't want to look like I'm trying too hard. There is no reason to change the dress. It's not dirty or anything."

"You're making me nervous the way you keep chewing your fingernails. Stop it!"

Rose placed her hands in her lap.

"A cup of hot tea will soothe your nerves," Tulip said.

"Okay, but wait until *Mamm* and *Dat* leave to go visiting. It shouldn't be too long now. And we have to make those sandwiches, which I nearly forgot about."

Tulip giggled. "Me too. Anyway, that won't take long. I'll go down and put the teakettle on and find out how long it'll be before *Mamm* and *Dat* leave. Then, I'll see what we have to put on those sandwiches." Tulip stood and headed for the door.

"Don't make it obvious, or they'll think we're up to something," Rose whispered.

"*Nee.* They already know we're going on a picnic." Tulip left the room before Rose could say anything further.

Rose was pleased she wasn't nervous when she was with Jacob. It was only when she thought about him that she felt anxious. Her mother had told her that whenever she felt like her head would explode, to take long deep breaths. She breathed in for ten counts and then out for ten counts. When she was on the third lot of repetitions, Tulip appeared before her and gave her a fright.

"They're leaving now." Tulip headed over to the window and looked down. "*Dat's* at the buggy and here comes *Mamm* right now. Now she's getting in."

Rose got off the bed and joined her sister at the window. "Do you think a hot tea will work? My stomach feels like a bundle of butterflies trying to escape."

"*Jah*, I'm sure it will. Come on." Tulip walked down the steps and Rose followed closely behind her.

As they sat drinking tea, Rose made a plan. "You keep Mark occupied and Jacob and I will go for a walk."

"How's that going to happen? Will you do that in the middle or the beginning or at the end of the picnic?"

"It'll have to be at the right time and I don't know when that'll be until it happens."

"Should we have a signal word, or something?" Tulip asked.

Rose pursed her lips. *"Nee.* We won't need anything like that. You won't need to instigate anything. When Jacob and I go for a walk, all you have to do is keep Mark talking and keep him away from us. The worse thing would be if he wants to go for a walk as well and he gets in the way. Do you know what I mean?"

"Ah, I see. I can do that." Tulip nodded.

"Good." Rose was so determined that nothing go wrong that while Tulip made the sandwiches, she carefully tutored her on what to do and say in every possible scenario that could possibly take place that afternoon.

When the girls heard a buggy, Tulip looked out the kitchen window. "It's them."

Rose jumped to her feet. "How do I look?"

Tulip looked her up and down. *"Wunderbaar."*

"Really? Or are you just saying that because you're my *schweschder* and you have to be nice?"

"You really do look good. Are you ready? We should go out and meet them rather than them come to the door. If they come to the door we'd have to ask them in and that wouldn't be allowed." Tulip bundled the wrapped sandwiches into a picnic basket and buckled it shut.

"I'm ready." Rose licked her lips. She was so nervous that her mouth was dry already.

"Do you want to carry the basket?"

"Nee, you do it," Rose said.

"Okay."

The men were out of the buggy already when Rose closed the front door behind her. Jacob was smiling so much that Rose found it hard to keep her eyes from him.

"Sit in the back with me, Rose," he called out. "Tulip can go in the front seat with Mark."

Rose was only too happy to sit close to him on the back seat. As they traveled to the park, Mark make certain that he was not left out of Rose and Jacob's conversation. That didn't bother Rose so much, as long as she could have some private time with Jacob later.

"This looks like a nice place to picnic," Mark said as he stopped the buggy at one end of the park.

"Looks good to me," said Tulip.

"Did you bring something to sit on, Mark? I totally forgot about that," Rose said.

"There should be a blanket in the back there just behind the seat."

Jacob reached behind them and found a blanket. "Got it," he said.

Rose hadn't needed to plan so intensely because after they'd finished eating, Tulip had gotten Mark talking and then Jacob sprang to his feet and suggested Rose go for a walk with him. Jacob had done it in such a way that Mark couldn't have done a thing about it if he'd wanted to. It also helped that Tulip was distracting him by talking quickly and barely drawing a breath.

As they started on their walk alone, Jacob said, "Those were lovely sandwiches, Rose. Did you make them?"

"Tulip made them."

"The bread was so tasty. Did you bake the bread?"

Rose giggled. "I can't take credit for that either. I don't do much of the cooking now that I work full time at the farmers market. It's my *mudder* and sisters who do that now. I help cook the evening meal when I get home and do a few chores in the morning before I leave for work, and that's it."

"Seems like it's been good for you to have a lot of sisters."

"I guess so, otherwise, I'd have to do more chores." Rose had to get the conversation off her and onto him. "Are you hoping your *onkel* might give you a full time job? I mean, is that the only thing that brought you here?" Rose asked.

He smiled at her and then looked down at his feet as he walked. "I'm thinking the time has come for me to find a girl. My parents are always telling me that's something I need to do before too long."

Rose laughed. "They sound like my parents. Well, my *Mamm*, at least."

"It's good to know I'm not the only one who's being influenced by their parents."

"That's probably true. I guess our folks are older and have more experience in things." Rose suddenly felt bold, and wanted to let him know how she felt. "So, is that what you're doing here—looking for a wife?"

He glanced down, and then looked in the distance as he answered, "To be honest, that's one of the main reasons I'm here. There are many lovely women back home, but there's not been one that I feel a connection with."

"That's sad."

"It's not sad, it's merely so. Anyway, I got to thinking I should do something about it." He flashed her a smile.

Rose liked a man of action. She was getting to like him more as they spoke. "I hope you'll find your trip is going to be worthwhile."

He slightly raised one eyebrow. "Maybe I already have."

Rose giggled at the way he smiled at her.

"Tell me, Rose, what is your relationship with my cousin?"

"You mean with Mark?"

"*Jah*, with Mark."

"He's just a friend."

"Does he know that?"

Rose swallowed hard. "Of course he knows that. We've been good friends for such a long time."

"I think he likes you as more than someone to pass the time with."

"*Nee*, he's always just joking around and we get along well. That's just how he is."

"That's good to know."

"Well, to be totally truthful, we had this dumb idea that he and I would pretend to be in a relationship so my mother would stop nagging at me."

He stopped walking and looked at her. "That sounds kind of dishonest."

"Oh, we never meant it to be like that. I can see how it sounds that way."

"I'd reckon it was Mark's idea."

Rose couldn't let Mark take the blame. "It was mine. It was a dumb idea and we never carried it through completely."

"I'm glad. Things like that have a way of backfiring on people. Dishonesty never pays."

"I agree with that. It was just a moment of silliness, nothing else."

They walked the next few steps in silence and then Jacob stopped in his tracks and Rose stopped along with him. "Rose, would you care to go on a buggy ride with me tomorrow?"

Rose hadn't expected this so soon. "I'd love to, but I can't because I work tomorrow."

"Perhaps I could collect you from work when you finish?"

"*Jah*, that might be a good idea. I'll let Mrs. Walker know that I have a ride home. It's the Walkers' stall and

Mrs. Walker brings me to work and takes me home. She'll be glad she doesn't have to do it."

"Shall I collect you from there at five?"

Rose nodded. "Five sounds good to me." She could see from Jacob's face that he was pleased she'd accepted his offer. Her plan with Tulip had worked brilliantly.

"Come on, we'd better get back to the others," he said. They turned around and as they headed back, Jacob started talking again. "I've got the idea that Mark likes you, as I said, but I think he's dating another girl. I find that confusing and a little odd. I never really understood Mark. He seems the old one out in his family."

"*Nee*, that's not possible. He would've told me if he had a girlfriend. We talk about everything."

"Everything?"

"*Jah.*" Rose nodded.

"Are you going to talk about me to my cousin?"

"*Ach nee.* I would never do that! I would never talk about personal things."

"Well, maybe Mark isn't telling you about things that are personal to him either."

Rose screwed up her face at the thought of Mark keeping something from her. It didn't seem likely. "I haven't heard that he is seeing anybody…," her voice trailed off. The thought of Mark dating someone and not telling her about it didn't sit well. And if Mark was dating someone, where was this mystery woman today?

Rose had grown used to the constant attention Mark had always given her and it was a little unsettling to think of that being taken away. Her mother always told Rose that she was the kind of person who wanted to have her cake and eat it too—and now she wanted to date Jacob, but she still wanted her special relationship with Mark. She had to admit that Mark's focused attention on her was kind of flattering. Suddenly she realized that she wouldn't be able to have that kind of relationship with Mark if she were dating his cousin, but it wasn't fair on Mark the way she occupied his attention.

"What are you thinking about right now, Rose?" Jacob asked.

She gave a little giggle. "You've got me thinking now. I'm thinking who Mark could have dated without me knowing. I normally get to find out about everything in the community. And I never thought Mark would have kept anything like that from me."

Jacob shrugged his shoulders. "Maybe I'm wrong. It's just the impression I got from a few things that Mark said. It's not unusual. A lot of couples keep relationships quiet until they're ready to go public. Everyone thought one of my cousins was single and then we found out he'd been dating a girl for two years. They announced their wedding and weeks later they were married." He snapped his fingers in the air. "As quick as that."

"I know it happens like that sometimes. My *bruder* just got married and they kept their relationship a secret for nearly a year before they told my parents they were getting married."

"Do you see? He could be secretly dating Tulip and you wouldn't know."

"What? Mark?" The thought of Mark and Tulip together was incomprehensible.

"Look at them over there now."

Rose looked to where Jacob was pointing. Mark and Tulip were sitting close together on the picnic rug, talking and laughing. She felt a pang in the pit of her stomach.

"Definitely not! Tulip is my *schweschder* and I know for a fact she's not dating Mark or anyone else."

Jacob laughed. "It's just an example. I didn't mean to worry you."

"I'm not worried. I'm not worried at all. It's just that Tulip tells me everything and so does Mark."

"People must trust you."

"I guess people who know me do."

When they'd walked two steps on, Jacob grabbed hold of Rose's arm and suddenly pulled her behind a tree. Now they were out of the sight of Mark and Tulip.

Chapter Thirteen

*But they that wait upon the LORD shall renew
their strength; they shall mount up with wings as
eagles; they shall run, and not be weary; and they
shall walk, and not faint.*

Isaiah 40:31

Rose giggled. "What are you doing, Jacob?"

"Before we go back and sit down to talk about nothing, I want to be honest with you."

"About what?"

"About how I feel about you. I never dreamed that
I'd meet a woman like you. I prayed to meet someone
and since the first time I saw you, I knew you were the
one—the one I've been waiting for."

Jacob's words were exactly what Rose wanted to
hear. This was everything Rose had ever imagined and
dreamed of. It had to have been love at first sight for
him too. He had exactly the same feelings for her that
she had for him. The image of him walking toward her
that first day, jumped into her mind.

"That's the same as I feel too," Rose said.

"If I hadn't come here, I'd have never met you. I need

to spend as much time with you as possible. Would your parents think it odd if I saw you again tomorrow night like we planned, or like we talked about?"

Rose giggled. "*Nee*. They want me to get married, but I don't want to do anything that would upset them, so I'll have to ask their permission."

"I meant for you to ask them. I would never go behind your parents' back with anything—not like Mark would."

Rose jolted her head back. "You're wrong about Mark. It wasn't like that. Anyway, it was my fault."

"Enough about him. I hope your folks like me."

"*Dat* likes you already, he said so, but they wouldn't like it if things moved too quickly. I've heard them talk about couples who get married fast. They talk about it as though they don't like it." Rose knew she had blushed when she mentioned marriage. "I mean, I didn't mean to say that we were getting married or anything like that."

"I think I know what you mean. Your parents are conservative and want things to take their proper time."

"That's it exactly. They want things to take their own time. You're very good with words, Jacob."

"That's only because I'm a little older than you."

Rose nodded.

"I've only got a few weeks, Rose, and then I have to head back. That's why I want to spend every moment together with you. Can you sneak out of the house tomorrow night after our buggy ride so we can spend some more time with each other?"

She tried to work him out. He said he didn't want to mislead her parents, but then again, sneaking out of the house was fine? "*Nee*. I wouldn't feel right about that. They would find out, and then I'd be in real trouble.

Then they'd punish me by making me stay in the house for a month."

"Wednesday night, then. Can I come and collect you on Wednesday night too as well as tomorrow night?"

"Maybe it would be better to go out Wednesday instead of both nights. And knowing my parents, they'll want you to come for dinner, so they can get to know you. How would you feel about that?"

"I can do that. I can come for dinner. Don't worry, I'll create a good impression."

Rose giggled. "I know you will. *Dat* already said he likes you from when he met you at the bishop's *haus*."

"*Gut!* You mentioned that already."

"Oh, I didn't mean to say it again. It was just that I want you to feel comfortable that my parents like you."

"Your *mudder* does too?"

"She hasn't mentioned you specifically because she doesn't know you."

"Well since your *vadder* likes me, my job is half done already."

Rose glanced out from behind the tree and saw that Mark was now looking around for them. "We should join them now. It wouldn't look good if we stayed away any longer."

"You're right. I wish we were here by ourselves. Mark is really getting on my nerves even though he's my cousin."

"Just get along with him. You'll like him once you get to know him better. He's quite funny."

"I know him well enough. I've seen him at least once a year even though we live far apart. Once a year is more than enough." He put his hand in the small of Rose's back. "After you, my lady."

Rose walked forward and the two of them joined Tulip and Mark.

"I'm glad you've come back," Mark said as they sat down.

"Yeah well, we got hungry again," Jacob said. "Are there any sandwiches left, or did you finish them all off, Mark?"

Mark glared at Jacob and then looked at Rose. "Picnics are about eating not walking."

Jacob started to say something, but Rose gently touched him on his arm and he stopped. When Jacob grunted, he looked away from Mark and looked from Tulip to Rose. "The sandwiches were tasty. *Denke* to you two girls for preparing it," Jacob said.

"Jah, denke," Mark said.

"There's more here." Tulip reached into the basket and pulled out more sandwiches. These ones were filled with pickles and roast meat. The first ones were a selection of chicken and ham. Each man took a sandwich and Rose handed everyone a paper napkin.

With more food and drink to occupy the two men, they each weren't focused on being irritated by the other.

While they ate, Rose knew she was smiling way too much, and hoped that Mark wouldn't ask what she was so happy about. Rose was thankful that Mark hadn't asked about the glow she knew must have been apparent on her face. He noticed though, she was certain of that.

When it was time to go home, Mark and Tulip carried the basket and blanket to the buggy ahead of Jacob and Rose, who dawdled behind.

Jacob moved himself closer to Rose. "I really want you to come out with me somewhere on Monday night as well as Wednesday night."

"I don't know."

"I've never met anyone like you, Rose. I can't stop

thinking about you all the time. I can't wait until Wednesday to see you again. It's far too long a time away. Please see me tomorrow night?"

Rose giggled. That was exactly what she wanted to hear. He felt the same as she.

"The only thing is that if I go out with you on both nights, my parents will want you to come for dinner soon. What do you think about that?"

"I'd already said I'd be happy to do that. I'd be delighted to do that any time your parents would like to invite me, or you'd like to invite me."

"Really?" She looked up into Jacob's soft brown eyes.

His lips drew upward at the corners. "Why are you so surprised?"

Now she knew he was serious about her. She couldn't tell him she was surprised because it would show how insecure she was. "I'm not sure."

"What is your answer then about tomorrow night? Quick tell me before we get to the buggy. I don't want Mark to know what we're talking about."

"It's not a secret, is it?"

"*Nee*, of course not, but he has a habit of ruining things for me. It's not a secret if you say yes." He stopped still and she stopped walking too. Then he looked down into her eyes. "What do you say, Rose?"

"Come on you two. It'll be dark by the time you get to the buggy," Mark called out as he waited by the buggy with Tulip.

"See what I mean? Come on, Rose. It'll make me really happy."

"Okay."

"*Wunderbaar.* I'll collect you at eight tomorrow night."

Before Rose could say another thing, Jacob was striding toward the buggy and Rose hurried to catch up to him.

* * *

When Rose and Tulip arrived home, their mother and father were back from their visiting, and the twins were still at the singing. Rose whispered to Tulip that she wanted to tell her parents about going out with Jacob the next night and on Wednesday night. She desperately hoped they wouldn't have a problem with that. Tulip offered to make herself scarce in her bedroom.

Her father was on the couch reading the newspaper, and her mother sat next to him, knitting. When Rose sat down in front of them, they both looked up expectantly. "I just wanted to tell you that I'm going out with Jacob tomorrow night and Wednesday night, if that's okay."

Her mother got in quickly before her father could say anything, "That's fine. I'm pleased to see you're getting out more. That's all I wanted."

When Rose looked over at her father for a sign of approval, he smiled and nodded, which was his way of saying he had no problem with it. That went a lot easier than she thought it would. "Okay then. I might have an early night. Oh, unless you want me to pick up the girls from the singing, *Dat*?"

"*Nee*, I'll get them. I'll give them a couple more hours."

She rose to her feet. *"Gut nacht."*

"Gut nacht, Rose," her mother said.

"Night, Rose," her father said as she hurried up the stairs.

Rose burst into Tulip's room and told her the good news that she was allowed to see Jacob on both Monday and Wednesday nights.

When everyone was home for dinner the next night, Nancy was worried that Rose was too interested in Jacob and they didn't really know him as they'd know a man from their own community. She left the girls to finish cooking the evening meal in the kitchen while she sat beside her husband on the couch.

"Rose is going out with Jacob after dinner," she said to Hezekiah as he read the paper.

"I know." He put the paper down in his lap and looked up at her. "You were fine with that last night when she asked us."

"I know, but since then I've got to thinking about things, that's all. Do you think she'll invite him for dinner soon?"

"Ask her to, if that's what you want."

"Don't you?"

"*Jah.* I'd like to get to know him better if Rose likes him as much as she seems to."

Nancy rubbed her neck. "*Nee,* I'll wait for her to ask me if he can come to dinner."

"As you wish."

"Well, what do you really think should happen?"

"I think I want to read the paper." When she sighed, he added, "You worry too much about things, Nancy. You were worried that she was never going to get married and now she's interested in a man, you worry about that too."

"Only because we don't know him that well."

"We know the Schumachers."

"*Jah,* we know them, but not their extended family."

"If you're worried about it, ask her to invite him to dinner. Simple! And that will stop you worrying so much."

"It's not as though I'm worried. It's not unreasonable to be concerned."

Hezekiah gave a low chuckle. "No matter what you call it, it's still the same thing."

"You're probably right. Over dinner, I'll suggest she invite him one night this week, or perhaps next week. Given her history of short relationships, it could even be over by next week, or even tomorrow."

Hezekiah laughed seeming to find what she said particularly funny. "I thought you didn't believe Mark and she were having a relationship."

Tugging with agitation on her *kapp* strings, Nancy said, "I don't know. She's very secretive. I hope all the girls aren't going to be like this. My hair will go more gray, grayer than it is already."

Hezekiah shook his head.

"What was that for?" Nancy asked. The approval of her husband meant everything to her and she didn't like it when they disagreed about things.

"Nothing."

He had a definite gleam in his eye as though he were amused about something.

"Tell me what you think is so funny."

He took a long deep breath, and then said, "I don't think she's secretive at all. She's not sneaking out to see anyone or lying to us. Now if she did, I would say she was a secretive or a deceitful person, but she's not doing that. You need to calm down and stop expecting the worst of situations."

Nancy bit her lip. "Is that what I'm doing?"

"I think it's just because you're over anxious and want the best for our girls. Trust in *Gott* and He will look after them and find them good husbands."

"You're right. *Jah*, I know you're right." There was a sudden clang in the kitchen, which sounded like a large saucepan had been dropped on the floor. Then an argument broke out between the girls. "I better get in there and supervise, or I'll have no kitchen left." She stood up and then leaned down and gave her husband a quick kiss on his cheek before she hurried off to the kitchen.

Nancy decided not to mention anything to Rose about inviting Jacob to dinner. Not tonight. She would wait to see if she also went out with him on Wednesday night like she'd planned. It wasn't as though she was thinking the worst, like Hezekiah said, but it was very likely Rose might cancel Wednesday night.

Rose was nervous about her buggy ride with Jacob. Earlier in the day at the markets, Mark had let her know that Jacob had asked to borrow his buggy to take her out. That was the only comment Mark had made about her going out with his cousin.

The twins teased her a little bit about Jacob over dinner, but after their father cleared his throat and glared at them, that was the end of that. Then their mother pointed out that Rose would get out of cleaning the kitchen and doing the washing up that night, and that made the twins grumble about the unfairness of being the youngest.

When Rose heard the buggy coming to the house, she was delighted. Not only would she get away from the twins' constant chatter and complaints, she'd get to be alone with Jacob.

"Bye, everyone," Rose called over her shoulder before she headed out the door. She got to the buggy before Jacob had a chance to jump down.

"Hi, Rose," he said in a deep manly voice as she climbed in next to him.

"Hi."

He turned the buggy around and set off down the

driveway. "I've got a lovely new buggy at home. It's embarrassing to collect you in a rickety buggy like this."

"It's fine. There's nothing wrong with it."

"Nothing wrong with it except it's fit for the scrap heap—the junk yard."

"It gets Mark to where he needs to go. That's all that concerns him. He's a practical man."

"Well, enough talk about Mark. You see him every day and I'm sure that's enough." He chuckled. "You must think I'm a dreadful person the way I speak about Mark sometimes."

"*Nee*, I don't. I know you don't mean it."

"I don't. I'm just fearful that you might like him if I'm totally honest with you. I guess that's immature. I'm working on being a better person because you deserve the best."

Rose was delighted that he was showing honesty as well as vulnerability. "*Denke.* That's a nice thing to say."

"It's true."

She hoped that meant he was going to stay longer. "How did you like your day at work?"

"Making buggies is nothing like I thought it would be."

"Do you like it better than upholstery?"

He leaned toward her and corrected her. "You mean upholstering?"

Rose giggled. "I don't know the right way to say it. I meant whatever it was that you used to do."

"I don't know that either of those things suit me, but I'm thinking of sticking with the buggy making for a little longer. I'm starting to like it here." He shot her a dazzling smile.

"I hope you'll stay a long time."

"Would you like to go back to the park where we

were yesterday? I noticed that it had lights and a walking trail. It would be a perfect place."

"I'd like that."

"I don't want to keep you out too long tonight. I figured out that your parents might not let you go out again on Wednesday night if they think I've kept you out too late tonight. Wednesday will be our real date night."

"I'm sure that will be fine with them, whatever time I get home."

"You might not know your parents as well as you think. I'm telling you now, they wouldn't be fine if you got home too late."

Rose wondered how many girls he'd been out with and how many parents had been cross with him for bringing them home late. She didn't ask because she didn't want to know.

When he stopped the buggy at the park, he stepped out and raced around to help Rose down before he secured his horse.

She loved the feel of her hand enclosed in his strong hand. He let go of her sooner than she wanted him to because he had to secure his horse to the post. To her delight, he took hold of her hand once more as they wandered onto the path.

"It's such a beautiful night," she said staring up into the starry sky.

"It's a beautiful night because I'm with you," he said and then released her hand to put his arm around her shoulder. Then he pulled her close to him.

She was taken aback a little at the suddenness of his movements.

"Are you okay?" he asked holding her firmly.

"*Jah*, I am."

"Me too."

They both laughed. They walked the next few minutes in silence.

"Why don't you put your arm around my waist?" Jacob suggested.

It didn't feel right, but Rose put her arm around him just the same. This was something she wasn't used to and it was the closest she'd been to a man. At the same time, it felt good.

"That's more like it," he said. "I'm so glad I met you, Rose."

"Me too."

"I have a serious question for you." He stopped abruptly and turned his body to face her causing her hands to fall down by her sides.

"What is it?"

"How do you really feel about me?"

She gulped and didn't know how to answer. What if she told him how much she liked him and he didn't like her as much? The last thing she wanted was to embarrass herself or have him laugh at her. Pushing nerves aside and hoping God would reward her honesty, she said, "I like you."

"Like?"

"*Jah*, I do."

"*Gut* because I like you an awful lot." He started walking again. "I see good things in our future, Rose." He pulled her tighter toward him.

She put her arm lightly around him where it had been before. "Like what?"

He glanced down at her. "Marriage, of course. What do you think about that?"

"That sounds good."

"Don't get me wrong, I'm not asking you just yet, but

if things keep going as well as they have been, I will ask you to marry me. How does that make you feel?"

"It makes me feel very happy."

"That's just how I want you to feel." He stopped again and then he slid both hands down to take hold of hers. Now he was looking down into her eyes. "You're so beautiful, Rose. One of the most beautiful girls I've ever seen. You're so pale and delicate, like a true rose."

Embarrassed and feeling heat rising in her cheeks, Rose went to walk away, but he wouldn't let her hands go.

"I mean it," he said.

He spoke with such intensity that Rose became a little nervous.

"I really want to kiss you right now," he said letting go of one of her hands. With his fingertips, he pushed back her prayer *kapp* and took hold of some loose strands of her hair.

Rose had no idea what he was about to do next. She was surprised when he leaned forward and smelled her hair. He was so close that Rose could smell his musky masculine scent. She desperately wanted him to kiss her, but at the same time, wanted to reserve her first kiss for her future husband. Right now, she didn't know for certain if he was the one. Fearing that he would kiss her, she stepped back before he could do so.

"What's wrong? Have I offended you?" He took a step back.

"Not at all. We should probably head back now."

"Normally I would say no, but we've got Wednesday night to look forward to." Hand-in-hand they walked back to the buggy under the moonlight.

It was the first romantic night Rose had ever had.

"Are you all right, Rose? Am I moving too fast with our relationship?"

"*Nee*, not at all. I'm looking forward to Wednesday night."

"Me too."

Their ride home was fairly quiet with neither of them speaking very much.

When they arrived at Rose's house, Jacob said, "Should I come in and say hello to your parents?"

"*Nee*. They're not expecting you to."

"Maybe I should walk you to the front door."

"I'm fine." Rose quickly got out of the buggy in case he tried to kiss her. When she was out completely, she turned back to face him. "I'll see you on Wednesday night."

"*Jah*, I'll be here at eight. *Gut nacht*, Rose. I won't be able to think about anything else until I see you again."

Rose giggled and said a quick goodbye before she turned and headed to the house. Her parents were awake and waiting for her. When she walked through the front door, they were sitting together on the couch and looked up as she closed the door behind her.

"You're early. Did things go alright?" her mother asked.

"Wonderfully well. I'm so looking forward to Wednesday night." Rose sailed past them and headed up the stairs pleased that they didn't ask anything further.

The next day, and the following day, Mark was strangely quiet. Rose made no comment about it to him because she knew he was upset about her seeing Jacob. Rose wanted nothing to ruin her Wednesday night with Jacob because he'd said that Wednesday night would be special. Even though it was far too soon and she didn't really know him, Rose daydreamed about Jacob asking him to marry her. It would be wonderfully romantic if they both knew so soon after meeting that they were destined for each other.

At last, Wednesday night arrived and as Rose waited on the couch to hear the *clip-clopping* of horse's hooves, her mother sat down beside her.

"Since after tonight you would've been out with Jacob twice, it would be nice to invite him to dinner. Your *vadder* and I would like to get to know him better."

It was no surprise to Rose that her mother said that. She'd been expecting she would be asked to invite him to dinner. "Sure. I'll ask him. Any particular night?"

"Before you go out with him again. It doesn't matter which night."

Rose leaped to her feet when she heard the buggy. "*Jah*, I'll ask, *Mamm*. That's him now." After she had grabbed her black shawl by the front door, she headed out of the house.

Her heart pounded when she jumped into the buggy beside him, and by the look on his face, he was just as pleased to see her.

"Hello, my sweet Rose."

"Hi."

"Let's go." He turned the buggy around and trotted the horse down the driveway.

"Where are we going tonight?"

"I don't know. Is there any particular place you'd like to go?"

As long as she was with him, she didn't care where they went. "Not really."

"I'll find a nice place where we can take a walk."

"That sounds good."

Jacob stopped the buggy on a deserted road. "This looks as good a place as any to take a walk in the moonlight. Just like we did on Monday."

"Okay."

He jumped down from the buggy and held out his hand to help Rose out. When she was on the ground, he kept hold of her hand. She liked the way he made her feel special. Pointing to the sky above, he said, "See the moon, Rose?"

Rose looked up at the moon that hung low in the sky—a crescent moon. "It's so beautiful."

He squeezed her hand as he stared at her. "Not half as beautiful as you."

When she glanced up at him, he stopped walking and looked into her eyes. Then he let go of her hand and placed his hand in the small of her back. He drew her close to him and lowered his head until she felt his warm breath tickle her face.

She stepped back. *"Nee."*

He took a pace forward. "What's wrong?"

"I want my first kiss to be when I'm married and not before then."

He stared at her in disbelief and then whispered, "Don't you see, Rose? I'm serious about you. If we both feel the same way, we will be married to each other."

"Really? You feel that way?"

"I do."

Once again, he put his hand behind her waist and this time he pressed her body against his. When he lowered his head, she turned her face and he was left to place his lips on her cheek. His lips were warm and soft. She wanted to kiss him on the lips, but had made the decision a long time ago to wait until her wedding day for her first real kiss.

He suddenly stepped back. "You're being quite ridiculous. Is there something wrong with you?"

"What do you mean?"

"If we're going to marry one day, why not kiss me now? Do you want to keep me waiting?"

Rose was upset at his outburst and didn't know what to say. Should she allow him to kiss her? She wanted to, so what was the harm? She stared at him open-mouthed wondering what to say.

"I'm sorry, Rose. I shouldn't have gotten angry. It's just that my feelings for you are strong and you're beautiful. I find you irresistible."

His words made Rose feel good, and he had apologized to her, which made her feel better. She had been taught to forgive so she did just that.

"Say something," he said.

"I forgive you."

He put out his hand and she took it. Together they walked down the moonlit road.

"Where shall we live when we marry? How would you feel about coming back to live with me?" he asked.

"I'd like to live close to my parents, but it doesn't really matter." She gazed up at him and he smiled.

After ten or fifteen minutes, they turned back to the buggy.

"Are you cold?" he asked.

"A little."

He put his arm around her and held her close. When they got by the buggy, he stopped. "Rose, I just need to kiss you on your beautiful lips. We need to seal our future with a kiss." Before she could respond, he pushed her against the buggy and brought his lips down hard against hers.

He was kissing her before she could stop him. She

knew that the right thing to do would be to push him away, but she didn't. As they kissed, he put his hands behind her back and pulled her hard into him until she found it hard to breathe. She finally pushed him away with both of her hands, and then gasped for air.

He laughed at her. "I think you liked that, didn't you?"

She wiped her moist mouth with the back of her hand. "I said I didn't want to kiss you and you made me."

"What's the difference if we kiss now or later?"

"It matters because you took away my choice." Rose wondered whether she was being silly about waiting for her wedding day to be kissed. Many girls didn't wait anymore.

He put his arm around her. "It's hard for a man to wait for a kiss from the woman he loves."

Her heart melted when she heard him say that he loved her.

"You do love me, don't you?" he asked.

"I do."

"Then that makes everything okay. Do you see that?"

Rose nodded, but would've felt better about things if she hadn't had her feelings overruled. "I suppose so."

"Anything we do is okay because we're in love, and soon, when it's time, we'll tell people."

"Okay." Rose nodded again pleased to be almost engaged and she knew that would make her mother thrilled.

"Let's walk some more." With his arm around her, they walked quite a distance in the darkness with the only light coming from the moon above them. "One day, I'll ask you to marry me. I'll ask you properly."

Rose would scarcely be able to wait. "My mother said to ask you to come to dinner."

He laughed. "See? Your parents like me—that should make you feel better about that kiss just now."

"I don't feel bad about it, it's just that I didn't expect it."

"You should have. All couples kiss and some do more. It's only the normal thing that everyone does."

If only someone had told Rose how things worked.

"How about tomorrow night for dinner at your folks'?" he asked Rose.

"*Jah*, that'll be fine. *Mamm* said any day would be okay."

"Come on. Let's head back," he said swinging her around to face the buggy.

When they arrived back at Rose's house, he pulled her close to him before she got out. This time, it was easier to kiss him because she'd already done so before.

"Don't forget I love you, Rose."

"I love you too, Jacob." She got out of the buggy and headed into the house wiping her mouth with her fingers. He was a little forceful, but perhaps that was what men were like when they were alone with a woman they were dating. At times like these, she could've done with an older sister who would've been able to give her advice.

Chapter Fourteen

*Be strong and of a good courage, fear not, nor
be afraid of them: for the LORD thy God, he it is
that doth go with thee; he will not fail thee, nor
forsake thee.*

Deuteronomy 31:6

Rose knew from the warm glow coming from the living room that everyone had gone to bed. There was a sole lamp burning, which had been left on, so she would have enough light when she got home. Once she was inside, she closed the front door behind her, and turned off the lamp before she carefully made her way up the now darkened wooden stairs to tell Tulip all about her night.

She leaned over Tulip's bed. "Are you awake?"

Tulip sat up. "*Jah*, I've been waiting up for you."

Rose told Tulip everything that was said between her and Jacob, leaving out the fact that she kissed Jacob not once but twice.

"I'm glad you're happy, but I don't like it how he asked you to sneak out," Tulip said. "It seems a little dishonest or something."

"That's because he's so in love with me that he wants

to see me all the time. Anyway, he'd forgotten he said that. He only mentioned it the once. You've got a good memory."

"I remember everything you tell me and I still think it's wrong that he asked you to do something he knew *Mamm* and *Dat* would be against."

"You'll understand when you're in love. Anyway, you shouldn't be so judgmental."

"Why's he moving so fast?" Tulip asked.

"We're in love and he's only got a few weeks before he has to go home. Unless I can persuade him to stay on for longer."

"Just be careful. You don't really know him."

"He's in the community, so he must be okay. He's coming for dinner tomorrow night."

"Okay. Then we'll see what *Mamm* thinks of him."

"Will you do something for me, Tulip?"

"What is it?"

"Will you work instead of me for a couple of hours tomorrow in the middle of the day? I want to surprise Jacob at the buggy workshop. It's not far from the markets."

"Okay. I'll go in with you in the morning."

"*Denke*, Tulip, I knew I could rely on you."

The next day just before lunchtime, Rose left Tulip to mind the stall while she went to surprise Jacob. She kept it quiet from Mark that she was surprising his cousin with a visit.

The taxi took Rose to the front of the buggy workshop and she walked into the office, which was in a large trailer. At one end, there was a large desk and filing cabinets and behind that desk was Marta Bontrager.

"Hello, Marta," Rose said as she walked forward,

glancing at two Amish women, who were sitting on chairs at the opposite end of the office.

"Hi, Rose. What can I do for you?"

"You have Jacob Schumacher working here and I was hoping I might have a word with him." Rose was secretly hoping that Jacob would be able to have lunch with her. Even if he couldn't, he'd love it that she'd thought to surprise him.

"Okay. Have a seat. I'll see if I can find him. He's popular today. I think he's due for a break soon."

Rose sat down while Marta left the trailer. With a sideways glance, Rose saw that one of the Amish women was young and the other was much older. They weren't from her community.

The young woman lurched forward. "Excuse me. I heard you were asking about Jacob?"

"*Jah*, do you know him?"

"Very well."

Rose studied the girl wondering if she might be Jacob's sister.

"How long have you known him for?" the girl asked.

"Only since he's been here. Are you a relation of his?"

The old woman sitting next to the girl spoke. "Jessica is Jacob's girlfriend. He said he was going to marry her and then he just up and disappeared. Now we found out he's here. And that's why we've come."

"Please don't!" Jessica said to the older woman.

"Well, that's how it is," the woman replied with a scowl.

Rose's heart sank. It didn't seem real. It couldn't be true. "You're his girlfriend?"

"I thought that's what I was until he disappeared. Now, I don't know what I am. That's what I've come here to find out."

Rose sat there dumbfounded. Now it was all clear. Jacob had wanted to see if there was another woman out there better suited to him before he made his commitment to marry Jessica.

Rose stood up. "It was very nice to meet you both." She rushed out of the small office before they could see the tears that had formed in her eyes. She'd allowed this man to kiss her. Now she felt violated by him. He'd cruelly used her.

The first person she wanted to rush to was Tulip, but that would mean she'd also have to see Mark and she wasn't ready for that.

I'm such a fool!

She decided to leave Tulip there for the rest of the day and Mrs. Walker could drive her home. Tulip wouldn't mind a bit when she explained what had happened.

Nancy Yoder was in the midst of sewing her daughters some new prayer *kapps* when Rose walked into the house, slamming the front door behind her.

"Rose! I didn't expect you home so soon. Did you leave Tulip at the markets?" She looked around and Rose was nowhere to be seen, but she heard her footsteps trudging up the wooden steps.

After giving Rose a little time alone, she made a cup of hot tea and took it up to her. Nancy gently knocked on the door, opened it, and saw her daughter in bed with tears flooding down her cheeks.

"What's wrong?" She knew in her heart Rose was crying over Jacob.

"Nothing!"

Nancy moved forward and placed the cup and saucer down on the nightstand. She sat on the end of the bed. "I can see there is something wrong."

"I'll not talk about it, *Mamm*."

"Is it about Jacob?"

Rose sat higher in the bed, licked her lips and then brought her knees up to hug them. "He's got a girl-friend."

Nancy couldn't stop the gasp that escaped her lips. *"Nee!"*

"Jah! And she's here! She followed him over here and she's with an older lady who might be her *mudder*. It was all such a shock."

"How did you find out?"

"I met them. I went to surprise Jacob where he worked and Jessica, that's his girlfriend, and the older lady were sitting there waiting for him too."

"Nee! That's a horrible thing."

"She said they were to be married and he just walked out on her and came here. I think he was looking around to make sure he was making the right decision. Like a boat setting sail out on the water. He wanted to make sure he was sailing in the right direction."

"Your *vadder's* been talking to you about sailing again?"

"How did you know?"

"It sounds like something he would say. He often talks about sailing and boats when he's trying to explain things."

Rose grabbed her mother's arm. "What do I do now, *Mamm*?"

"Not everyone marries the first girl they go out with, Rose. Maybe he just didn't feel the girl was suited to him and there's nothing wrong with that."

"Maybe so, but I don't like that he was keeping the relationship going on while looking around for somebody else. He should've ended things with her first. From what she said, he just left her not knowing."

"He wanted to have his cake and eat it too."

"Exactly right." Rose nodded. "But I don't like being the cake."

Chapter Fifteen

And the Lord God said, It is not good that the man should be alone; I will make him an help meet for him.

Genesis 2:18

Nancy hated to see her daughter in so much pain and torment. She sat on the edge of Rose's bed looking into her green eyes in silence for a few moments before she spoke again. "Jacob needs to give you an explanation."

Rose held her head. "I don't know."

"*Jah*, you do. There are two sides to every story. Maybe this girl only told you half of what had gone on. Maybe Jacob *had* ended things with her and she hadn't accepted it. You've got to give him a chance to explain. That's what adults do."

Rose shook her head. "I suppose you're right, but I can't see that the girl was making any of this up."

"Your *grossdaddi* always used to say that there are two sides to every story and the truth lies somewhere in the middle. Jacob sees things from his point of view and she sees things from her point of view and they're not the same."

Rose sighed and rubbed her eyes. "*Dat* says a person should stick to their word. If you say you're going to do something then you should do it. Jacob said he was going to marry her and then walked out on her just like that."

"Maybe she misunderstood what he said about their relationship. If you really like Jacob, you should listen to what he says about it when you ask him."

Rose stared at her mother. "Maybe the girl misunderstood and maybe she's one of those girls who thought she was in a relationship and she really wasn't."

"*Jah.* Maybe. Do you think so? It could be that Jacob wasn't at fault."

Nancy smiled trying to be encouraging until the truth was discovered. "It's quite possible. Talk to him and see what he says. He's still coming to dinner tonight, isn't he, and then you're going on a buggy ride?"

"*Jah*, if that's still on, and he's not spending tonight with his girlfriend."

"Don't be like that. If he comes here tonight, talk to him after dinner about what this young lady said, and see what he's got to say."

"Okay, I will."

"And don't be too hard on yourself, or on him. We all make mistakes."

"But shouldn't I be harsh on him? I don't want to make any mistakes choosing my husband."

"Nobody is perfect, Rose. Remember that."

"I know that. I'm not expecting my husband to be perfect, but I do need a man who sticks to his word. That's important to me. I need someone I can feel safe with."

"Drink your tea and then you'll feel better."

Rose looked down at the tea beside her. "*Denke, Mamm.* Maybe you're right and Jessica did misunderstand him. I'll wait to hear what he says."

"That would be a *gut* idea."

Nancy walked downstairs and out of the house, determined to get to the bottom of things. She went into the barn and made a couple of calls, intending to find the truth. She knew a couple of families who lived in Oakes County. Her first call was to Jean Davis, a woman she was sure knew everyone in Jacob's community.

Once Nancy opened her address book, she dialed Jean's number. The call was answered almost immediately.

"Hello, Jean. It's Nancy Yoder."

"Nancy! Is anything wrong?"

"*Nee.* I've called to ask you a couple of quick questions if you don't mind."

"I don't mind at all. What is it?"

Nancy said, "There's a young man who's arrived here who comes from your community. He's staying with his relations who are friends of ours. Rumor has it that he's got a girlfriend back there and I was wondering—"

"Jacob Schumacher?"

"*Jah*, how did you know?"

"I'm afraid it's true, Nancy. The poor girl's devastated. I know her *mudder* well and she told me just yesterday. They were keeping their relationship quiet and Jessica thought things were going well and they'd even spoken of marriage and he disappeared without saying a word."

'Spoken of marriage' was quite different from being engaged. "I'm sorry to hear that," Nancy said.

Jean continued, "And Jessica had to find out where he'd gone from Jacob's parents. It had to be embarrassing for her."

"There's no doubt it would've been."

"Why are you asking, Nancy?"

Nancy swallowed hard. She didn't want to lie and neither did she want to gossip. If poor Jessica found out that her daughter and Jacob had been dating, that could quite possibly escalate a storm. That's not what she wanted to do.

"Some people had some questions, that's al!. Then, Jessica's here with another lady, and I just wondered. I hope you don't mind me asking you those questions."

"*Nee*, not at all. The lady she's with would most likely be her aunt, Becca."

"*Denke.*" Nancy talked a little bit more about other things before she hung up. She'd told her daughter to give Jacob the benefit of the doubt, but now she knew that he'd walked out on that poor girl without an explanation. That wasn't the kind of man she wanted her daughter to marry. She wanted Rose to marry someone true to his word, just like Rose's father.

As Nancy walked toward the house, she made up her mind that she'd allow Rose to figure things out for herself. She hoped that Rose would tell Jacob that she didn't want to see him anymore. Rose had to grow up sometime and this adult decision would help turn her into a woman.

Chapter Sixteen

*I will say of the Lord, He is my refuge and my fortress:
my God; in him will I trust.*

Psalm 91:2

Rose made sure she was right there at the front gate
to meet Tulip when Mrs. Walker dropped her at home.
When Tulip got out of the buggy, Rose rushed forward to
explain to Mrs. Walker that she had been unwell and had
gone home. Then she walked with Tulip to the house and
told her everything that had happened during the day.

"So what's your opinion?" Rose asked.

"I feel sorry for Jessica, but if he'd changed his mind
about her, what was he to do? You can't marry someone
just because you feel sorry for them. He made a mistake, and now he likes you. That's how it seems to me."

"*Jah*, but didn't he—I mean, shouldn't he have told
her how he felt before he just up and left? She was left
to wonder what was going on and now she must be so
embarrassed."

"Sometimes we do things without thinking. You
shouldn't be so harsh on him, but at the same time you
have to be careful."

"Do you think I'm being harsh?" What would Tulip think if she told her how he'd forced her to kiss him? Rose couldn't bring herself to tell her sister that!

"You're a perfectionist, Rose, but sometimes life and people aren't how you want them to be."

"I'm not expecting Jacob to be perfect, but there are a few principles that I want the man I'm going to marry to have."

"And who's to say that he doesn't have all of those? You've only known him for a little over a week. You should wait at least a few months before you start assessing him."

"Do you think so? I thought you'd decide you didn't like him, and would tell me not to see him anymore."

"I don't think it's about that. I think you've built up an image of what you want in a man—this whole perfect man, and you've made that man too idealistic. Real people have flaws and if you want a real husband rather than one who only lives in your mind, you'll have to accept a few imperfections."

"*Jah*, the man I will marry will be everything I want him to be, or I just won't get married. If he wasn't perfect, why would I marry him?"

Tulip giggled. "Don't say that around *Mamm* or she'll have a heart attack."

Rose laughed a little. "I'm glad I can talk with you. You might be right, he could have a reasonable explanation for everything."

"Exactly. This girl could've thought the relationship was serious, more so than it was. They might have only been on one date together and she expected him to marry her."

"You could be right. But the woman with her agreed with everything she said."

"It's possible that the woman has only heard Jessica's side of things."

Rose nodded. Her sister and her mother were saying the same kind of things.

"Let's go and help *Mamm* with the dinner," Tulip said. "But you didn't ask me how work was today."

"How was it?" Rose asked.

"It was good. It got really busy around lunchtime and then toward the end of the day it was quiet."

"That's how it usually is."

"I think Mark's in love with you," Tulip said with a grin.

"Do you think so? I knew he liked me a bit. Love is a strong word."

"He talked of little else in between customers."

Rose knew it was true. His teasing and jokes about them getting married one day had an element of truth in them, from his side. That's what he wanted—for them to marry.

"So?" Tulip stared at her.

"You know I don't like him in that way. I'm in love with Jacob."

"I know, but Mark is so nice."

"*You* marry him, then." Rose giggled.

"You wouldn't mind?" Tulip asked. "I mean, truly wouldn't mind?"

Rose glanced at her sister's face as they walked up the driveway to their house. "Go ahead. You'd make a nice couple." Rose suddenly had a hollow feeling in the pit of her stomach. It would be weird if her sister married her good friend. She'd grown used to him and his company. Things wouldn't be the same in their friendship if Mark were dating Tulip.

"Jacob is coming for dinner tonight, isn't he?"

"*Jah*, he's coming here and then we're going on a buggy ride after dinner. I'm going to make dessert and show him what a good cook I am."

"That would be a good idea. When do you think you might get married?"

"He's here for a few weeks, and then I guess we'll write to each other. After that, he might ask me to come and visit him."

Tulip giggled. "You've got it all worked out."

"I have. I hope he'll want to come back here to live though. I don't want to live in a strange place where I don't know anyone."

"You'll make friends and besides, it's not that far away."

"Maybe he'll propose to me in a letter. That would be romantic, and then I'll have it to keep forever, and one day I could show our *kinner*. That is, if he gives me a good explanation tonight about Jessica."

Rose paced up and down waiting for Jacob to arrive for dinner. Then, when she heard the *clip-clopping* of horse's hooves and saw that it was him heading toward the house, she opened the front door and went outside to meet him.

He gave her a wave and then brought the horse closer to the house. When he got out of the buggy, she saw he looked upset. Maybe he'd had a talk with Jessica and sorted things out. She hoped that Jessica wasn't too upset and that he'd let her down gently.

"Hello, Rose."

"Hello. Is everything alright? You don't look too happy."

He looked down at the ground and then took a couple

of steps before he looked back up at her. "There have been some developments."

"*Jah*, I know. I was there at your work today and I ran into Jessica."

"So you know?"

Rose nodded. "I do."

He gave a relieved sigh. "That's good. I thought you'd be upset with me."

He was here, so he must've sorted things out with Jessica, she thought. "There are always two sides to every story. I'm not upset with you at all. I only hope that Jessica isn't upset."

His eyebrows drew together. "Why would she be upset?"

"When you told her that you weren't going to marry her."

He looked away and then shuffled his foot, rolling a couple of pebbles back and forth under his shoe. He looked up at her. "Jessica and I had a long talk today, and to make a long story short, we're getting married."

Rose felt all life drain from her. It couldn't be true. "What are you talking about? She said you just left her and came here. She said you were going to marry her and then you changed your mind, or something."

"I had to clear my head. I had to think what I really felt about her before I made the next step. I'm only here to tell you in person. I'm not here to stay for the meal."

Rose's fingertips flew to the sides of her head. "You wanted to see who else was out there? Was that it?"

"I'm sorry, Rose. I never meant to hurt you."

"We kissed! You kissed me!"

"It was only a kiss—nothing more."

"I told you I didn't want to." She was hurt, desperately hurt. He preferred someone else. Nothing he'd ever said was true. She scowled, not the slightest concerned about how unattractive her face looked in that moment.

He took a step toward her. "Rose, it's not like that, I honestly prefer you, but—"

"But what?"

"It's complicated."

"It's not complicated in the least. You chose her over me, so there's nothing difficult about that. I don't know what you're thinking by even coming here. I even made a special dessert for you. I'll throw it in the trash!"

"I won't come in. I didn't expect that I would be staying for dinner after I said what I came to say. I only came to tell you in person. Let your parents know I'm sorry, but…tell them I'm unwell. I'm sorry, Rose. I didn't… I didn't mean it to end like this. I didn't mean to hurt you. That was the last thing I wanted."

"What about all those things you said to me? Were you lying about everything?"

He looked down at the ground once more. "I can't answer that."

Rose stamped her foot. "You can't answer that because you were lying. Go! Leave my place now and never come back!" Rose turned to leave, but he caught her by her elbow and abruptly swung her around to face him.

"Rose, there are some things you don't know."

"Well, tell me."

"I can't."

"You forced me to kiss you and you said it would be okay because we'd be married. I wanted my first kiss to be on my wedding day, or at least with my husband, and you stole that from me."

He shook his head. "Grow up, Rose. You're not so special that a man would wait for you to kiss him. Maybe that's how things were two hundred years ago, but today a man needs more. More than a kiss, even."

Rose's jaw dropped open and she turned on her heel and stomped away without saying another word. Now she knew the truth. Jacob was just horrid, and she'd made an awful, terrible mistake.

Chapter Seventeen

Trust in the Lord with all thine heart; and lean not unto thine own understanding. In all thy ways acknowledge him, and he shall direct thy paths.

Proverbs 3:5-6

Minutes before...

From the kitchen window, Nancy watched her daughter hurry to meet Jacob outside. The scene brought her mind back to when she and her husband were getting to know one another. She'd told herself she'd never spy on her daughters, but she found herself doing just that.

"I'll set the table, *Mamm*," Tulip said.

"Denke." Nancy didn't want Tulip to see she was watching the young couple so she busied herself preparing for her daughter's boyfriend's dinner at the house.

When Tulip's back was turned, she glanced out the window again to see what looked like some kind of a disagreement. Nancy guessed there was more to the story of Jessica, the young woman who was visiting their community. Could he have chosen Jessica over her daughter?

It certainly looked that way from Rose's body movements and it looked like she was even yelling at him.

Now Rose headed to the house and Jacob was wasting no time getting back into his buggy. Nancy hurried to meet Rose at the front door. "What's happened? Where's Jacob?"

"He's not coming to dinner tonight, or any other night. We're through—it's over!" Rose burst into tears before she ran up the stairs.

Nancy stood there frozen, not knowing what to do. She hadn't had any dramas like this with her sons. The sound of Rose's bedroom door slamming echoed through the house.

Tulip ran out of the kitchen. "What's going on?"

Nancy swung around to face her. "Rose and Jacob had some kind of argument."

"I'll go to her."

"*Nee*, don't. I'll give her a few minutes and then I'll talk with her."

"What's happening? Isn't Jacob coming to dinner now?" Daisy asked as she also ran from the kitchen to her mother.

"Did they have an argument?" Lily yelled out from the kitchen.

"Hush!" their mother said, not wanting Rose to hear them discussing her. It'd only upset her more. She looked at Daisy. "He's not coming to dinner now. Go and tell your *schweschder* to be quiet."

"Which one? Rose or Lily?"

"Lily, of course. Now's not the time for game playing. You know who I meant."

Daisy's mouth turned down at the corners as she flounced back into the kitchen.

"He's not coming now," Daisy yelled to her twin on the way.

"*Gut!* There'll be more food for us," Lily called back.

Nancy shook her head. "Hush, all of you."

"*Mamm*, it's best if I go up and talk with her," Tulip said over the top of the twins' sniggers.

Nancy was a little disturbed that the twins seemed to be enjoying the drama. She looked at Tulip, her second oldest daughter, and put her hands on her shoulders and looked her directly into her face to hold her attention. "This is something that is a *mudder dochder* thing. I'll have a talk with your *vadder* when he gets home, which should be soon, and then I'll go to her. Until then, help me with the dinner, *jah*?"

Rather than answer, Tulip pulled her mouth to one side.

"Trust me, Tulip, I know what I'm doing," *Mamm* said taking hold of Tulip's arm and guiding her back to the kitchen.

"I could talk to her," Lily suggested.

"*Nee!*" Tulip and their mother said at the same time.

"That's a little harsh," Daisy said.

"It's okay, I'm used to being left out of things," Lily replied stifling a giggle.

"Stop it, both of you!" Nancy wagged a finger at her twin daughters. "This is a serious thing. Rose is upset, and you're being very unkind."

"He was too handsome anyway," Daisy said in a small voice.

Nancy frowned. "What has that got to do with anything?"

"The more handsome a man is, the less kind he is," Daisy said which made Lily giggle. "It's true. I know these things," Daisy insisted.

"You'll marry an ugly man and have ugly *kinner* then," Lily replied.

Daisy stuck her nose in the air. "As long as he loves me, I don't care."

Nancy sighed in despair. Her two sons had been so easy to deal with and she hadn't appreciated it at the time. They'd found wives without any problems. Something gave Nancy the feeling that all of her girls would be challenging in the romance sector of life.

A horrible thought occurred to Nancy and she clutched at her throat. What if her four daughters all remained single? She would be an old lady with four middle-aged daughters still living in her house squabbling and bickering. When would she have a chance to be alone and enjoy her last years with Hezekiah? "All of you concentrate on cooking."

"It's all done," Lily said with her arms raised.

"The table's still not set. You know how your *vadder* likes his dinner as soon as he gets home."

To Nancy's relief, the three girls found something else to talk about other than Rose's disaster.

As soon as Nancy walked into Rose's room, she looked up from her seated position on her bed. "I'm never going to marry anyone—ever. I'll never be able to trust anybody. I trusted Jacob and look what happened. He lied to me. He told me how much he liked me, and he knew it was all lies. He didn't mean a word of it."

"What happened?"

"He's going to marry Jessica. That's what happened. After telling me he loved me. I don't know how Jessica can trust him after he walked out on her."

Nancy gasped and put her hand on her heart. "That's a surprise."

"Why would she take him back? It doesn't make sense."

"She probably has forgiveness in her heart."

Rose's green eyes flashed. "I have none! I will never forgive him and I will never marry anyone because I'll never be able to trust anyone ever again as long as I live."

"Rose, you can't mean that. You're just upset."

"Why would I love and put myself at risk for being hurt again?"

"You only knew him for a couple of weeks or less. It can't have been real love. You can't tell me you could have fallen in love with him in that short amount of time."

"I didn't know there was a time limit on love, *Mamm*."

"I don't know that there is, but you wouldn't have had time to find out what kind of person he was."

"Well I certainly know what kind of person he is now! He's a person who can't be trusted, and if I'm so dumb and easily fooled who can I ever trust again?"

Her mother pushed some strands of hair away from Rose's face.

"Anyway, *Mamm, denke* for coming to talk with me, but I'd rather be alone if that's okay."

"Of course it is. I understand. I'll bring some dinner up to you."

"*Nee*, don't." Rose shook her head and then ripped off her prayer *kapp* and held it with both hands. "The last thing I feel like is food."

"You've got to keep your strength up, Rose."

"You can bring the food up if you want, but I won't eat it. It'll only be wasted." Rose lay down across her bed, wiggled herself lower, and pulled the covers over her head.

* * *

The next morning, Rose had to go back to work. She couldn't miss two days in a row. And she'd quite possibly feel better back in her normal routine. Some time with Mark would make her feel happy again. She wondered what Mark would say about his cousin and Jessica. Rose only hoped Jacob would go home sooner than he'd planned. It would be hurtful and embarrassing to see him out and about with his girlfriend. What a fool she made of herself by liking him.

As soon as Mrs. Walker let her out at the farmers market, she saw Mark in the distance and hurried toward him. When she got closer, he saw her and waited for her.

"I'm so sorry I was mean to you, Mark," she blurted out.

"*Nee*, it's me who should apologize to you. I had no right to tell you what to do."

"You've heard about Jacob?"

"Have you?" Mark asked.

"He told me he's marrying Jessica. After he told me..."

Mark frowned and his eyes narrowed.

Rose's shoulders drooped. "Never mind. It's just a weird thing that's happened."

"It is, and I'm sorry things didn't work out for you and Jacob. I know you liked him."

Rose sighed. "At least I know now that I'll never marry."

"Never marry anyone?"

"Never."

"You can't mean that, Rosie."

"I do."

"Unless it's to marry me, right?" Mark asked jokingly.

Rose was pleased they were back to the old Mark and

Rose. She had to giggle at his words and the silly expression now on his face. "I'm sorry to disappoint you, Mark. I won't even marry you."

"You'll change your mind one day. I'll grow on you; you just wait and see. I'll grow on you like ivy grows on a tree—slowly but surely, never giving up."

"We'll see." Rose giggled again.

During the day, Rose learned that Jacob and Jessica were leaving that day, along with Jessica's aunt, to head back home.

Rose was relieved that she wouldn't have to see them. She felt foolish to have believed everything Jacob had said to her. Not only had he robbed her potential husband of her first kiss, he'd robbed her of her desire to marry.

Chapter Eighteen

I will lift up mine eyes unto the hills, from whence cometh my help. My help cometh from the Lord, which made heaven and earth.

Psalm 121:1-2

When Rose arrived home from work that night, her gloomy mood returned. Somehow everything reminded her of Jacob.

Rose knew she was in a depression and she couldn't pull herself out of it. She had been dumped; she had been cheated by the man she thought she would marry, and no one except Tulip understood.

The twins weren't sympathetic because they didn't understand how she could develop real feelings for someone in such a short space of time. They poked fun at her and told their mother that Rose was just trying to get attention. Her mother was worried about her, and her father always stayed out of what he called, 'girl problems.'

After dinner that night while they were washing up, Rose's mother told her she wanted to have a chat with her. The twins and Tulip were sent to sit with their father in the living room.

"I'm troubled about you, Rose."

"Why? I'm fine. There's nothing to worry about." Rose dried the plate too many times back and front until she noticed her mother staring at her. She quickly put the plate with the other dry ones.

"You're not yourself."

"I am, I'm the new me. This is how I am now."

"Don't be like that. Just because you've had one bad experience with a man doesn't mean you're never going to find someone who suits you."

"I'm not going to marry, and I don't have to. Even the Bible says that people don't need to marry if they don't want to. I think it was Paul who said it was preferable not to marry but if people had to do so, then it was okay. So, I'm going to be like Paul and stay single. It's a Godly choice."

"Leave the dishes. Let's sit at the table. I'll have the twins do it."

Rose sat down and her mother sat opposite.

Then her mother's fingertips drummed on the kitchen table. "You're not making your decision out of a Godly choice. You're making it out of hurt. Besides, Paul was a man. Maybe things were different for men and women back then. Those were different times and in a different culture."

"Ask *Dat* about it. He'd know. I'm sure it's okay for a woman just as it would be for a man not to marry. No one can force me; it's my choice."

"I just want you to be happy, and in an ideal situation you would be happily married."

"That's not what I want anymore, *Mamm.* I thought I did, but it only leads to disappointment. I want to be happy and being in love is okay when it's *gut,* but I don't think I've ever been so low. I feel as though there's no point to life almost."

"Honey, that was just one man. They're not all like that."

Rose swallowed hard. "He was the *only* man for me and then it all turned bad."

"Is he the only man you want?"

Rose nodded. "He is."

"Do you think you should find out if he and Jessica are still engaged? They had a rocky relationship, so maybe they're off again. I could make some calls and—"

"*Nee*, I don't like him anymore! I wouldn't marry him now. He could change his mind about me just as easily as he changed his mind about her. The perfect man for me would never have walked away and left me."

Her mother was silent for a while before she spoke again. "Your *vadder* and I have talked about it and we've arranged for you to speak with Bishop John and his *fraa*."

Rose leaped to her feet knocking the chair over as she did so. "Talk to the bishop about my personal things?"

"We're worried about you. And we both think it's best that you speak with him and tell him how you feel."

Rose picked up her chair and sat back down. Maybe talking it over with someone would help her sort out her feelings. "I guess it wouldn't hurt if that's what you want me to do. But I'm not sure what you think it's going to accomplish. I can't be the only girl in the community who has chosen never to marry."

"It's not only that. You just don't seem to be yourself."

"And what do you think the bishop can do about that? I'm upset, that's all."

"He has a lot of experience about everything—all

life's situations. He'll give you some good advice, I'm sure."

"I can't imagine what about."

"See that there—that attitude? That 'don't care' attitude? I think you're feeling sorry for yourself. You've never spoken out like that to me before. You've always been so polite."

Rose didn't make a comment. No one cared about her, so why should she care about herself? "And when have you arranged for me to go and see them—the bishop and Olga?"

"On Thursday after you finish work. *Dat* will collect you from work and take you there. You can tell Mrs. Walker tomorrow that she won't need to collect you on Thursday night."

Rose shrugged, too tired to be bothered with arguing. "Okay, *Mamm.* Whatever you want."

The next morning, Rose couldn't wait to tell Mark that her parents were sending her to talk to the bishop and his wife. Mark had overprotective parents as well, and he'd have a good chuckle about it with her.

When Rose got to her stall, Mark was nowhere to be seen and he always arrived before she did. Instead of Mark, she saw his younger brother, Matthew.

"Matthew, what are you doing here?"

"I thought Mark would've told you. I'm taking over the store from him."

"What? Why?"

"He got an offer to learn the trade from *Onkel* Harry. He's going to be making buggies."

Rose frowned. Just when she really needed Mark, he'd left her. "Isn't that what Jacob was doing?"

"*Jah*, but Jacob has gone and…so it goes."

"Jacob and Jessica have gone now?"

"They left yesterday. Didn't you know?"

"I did. I was just making sure. Jacob told me they were leaving. I was just checking that they'd actually left."

"No one had heard about Jessica until she showed up here." Matthew laughed. "Jacob will be under the thumb soon if he doesn't watch himself."

"What?" Rose frowned. "What do you mean?"

"She snaps her fingers and then he goes running back home. He was supposed to be here for a few months." Matthew shook his head as though disgusted. "I don't know what happened there."

Rose kept silent and set about readying the stall for the day's trade. She tried to make the display as attractive as possible. Each day before she arrived or just after she arrived, one of the Walker boys brought the buckets of flowers in. The arranging of the flowers was left to Rose.

She glanced over at Matthew and knew it wouldn't be as much fun working there without Mark, she knew that right away.

Rose had been right—the day dragged by without her friend.

She wondered if Mark was angry with her. "Matthew, why does Mark want to work with your *onkel*?"

"I dunno. He doesn't have a lot of choices. He doesn't like to work in the dairy. That's why he chose to work here, and now he's gonna make buggies."

"I know he doesn't like to work in the dairy, but he never said a thing about wanting to make buggies."

Matthew shrugged his shoulders. "Like I said, I dunno. Maybe that's not his ideal thing, but we've all gotta work."

just that she'd missed him as one would miss the companionship of any good friend?

He picked up a jug, poured her a glass, and then handed it to her.

"Denke."

When he poured one for himself and took a sip, Rose wondered if he felt just as awkward as she did.

"I missed you today," he said.

"Me too. I missed talking with you too."

"We had a lot of fun. Well, not really fun, but having you there helped pass the time when things got quiet."

Had? Was their time together over just like that? She nodded and then looked down at the ground, wondering what to say.

"I'm sorry about the Jacob thing," he said.

"I'm over it now. There's no need to say anything. Things always turn out for the best."

"That's exactly right; they do." He nodded.

She smiled the way he said his last words with such enthusiasm.

"I hear your parents are forcing you to go to the bishop tomorrow night."

"What? How in the world did you hear that?" Rose asked.

"My aunt just happened to be at Bishop John's *haus* and overheard a conversation between him and his *fraa* about you going there."

Rose slapped a hand to her forehead while she tried not to spill the drink in her other hand. *"Ach,* that's so embarrassing. Did they say what it was about?"

"Nee. Don't you know?"

"My *mudder* thinks I'm in some kind of a depression. Only because I said that I won't get married."

"Well there's nothing wrong with that."

"I suppose that's right—it is a job. And what were you doing before you came here?"

"Working the dairy."

It was Rose's worst fear that Mark and she would grow apart. Now she would only see him at the young peoples' 'singings,' the fortnightly Sunday meetings, and the various social events. "When did he decide to work with Harry?"

"You sure ask a lot of questions about my *bruder*."

Matthew smiled at Rose and she knew he thought that she liked Mark. She did, but not in the way that Matthew might have thought.

He finally answered, "When he heard Jacob was leaving was when he said he'd work with Harry. Harry had been asking him for some time."

"Do you think you'll like this job?" Rose only asked because she had to talk about something other than Mark.

"Anything that will get me away from the dairy is good. The dairy is hard work. Not that I mind the work, it's just nice to have a change."

Mark and Matthew were fortunate to be the youngest of the Schumacher boys. The older ones had all worked in the dairy at some point. Rose considered that Mr. Schumacher must be pleased to have had so many boys to help with everything.

Toward the end of the day, Rose remembered that there was a volleyball game on that night. Normally she wouldn't attend, but tonight she'd go and hope that Mark would be there. Seeing his friendly face would make her feel better.

Chapter Nineteen

*Cast thy burden upon the Lord, and he shall sustain
thee: he shall never suffer the righteous to be moved.*
                                                    Psalm 55:22

The volleyball game was already under way when Rose
arrived with Tulip and the twins in tow. Before Rose
brought the family buggy to a complete stop, the twins
leaped out and ran off to join their friends.

"They'd be in trouble now if *Mamm* or *Dat* were
here," Tulip said, watching her younger sisters disap-
pear into the crowd.

"Don't worry about them. Can you see Mark anywhere? I can't wait to talk with him."

Tulip craned her neck as she looked at the group of
people. "*Jah*, I can see him now. He just got up to play."
Tulip turned to look at Rose. "What do you want to talk
with him about?"

"I want to know why he didn't tell me he was chang-
ing jobs."

"I don't know, but maybe you can ask him tonight."
Rose stepped out of the buggy. "I intend to." She

looped the reins over the fence and secured the horse.
Then together she and Tulip headed to join the onlookers.

Throughout the night, Rose avoided looking directly
at Mark. She could see him turning around trying to
catch her eye, but she deliberately didn't look back.

As soon as the games were over, Mark walked over
to her just like she had wanted. "I hoped you'd come
tonight, Rosie."

"I'm here."

He chuckled quietly. "I can see that. I'm glad."

"Well, did you win?"

"Volleyball?"

"Yeah."

"We won two games."

"Is that good?"

He laughed. "*Nee*. We played ten games and the teams
I was playing on only won two."

Rose couldn't wait to talk about his new job. "You
didn't tell me you were leaving the market stall."

"I didn't have time. It was a sudden last-minute thing
when Jacob left."

"Do you like making buggies?"

"I guess so. It's too soon to tell for certain. I've always wanted to have some kind of trade for myself. If
I'm going to raise a *familye* one day, I'll need to have
money to feed all those little mouths." Mark chuckled.

"It wasn't much fun today without you there."

"Yeah, I can imagine that. My *bruder's* a little dull."
Mark stared at her when she didn't laugh. "Can I get
you some soda?"

Rose nodded and together they walked to the re-
freshments table. For the first time ever, Rose wondered
whether she liked Mark as more than a friend. Or was it

Rose smiled at him. Finally someone understood her. "Do you think so?"

"I think it's a good decision."

"I'm glad you think so. I hope you're not the only one in the whole community who thinks that. And why do other people think it's any of their business?"

"Mmm, I don't think they do."

Rose was half waiting for him to say that she shouldn't marry anyone but him. That's what he would've said weeks ago, but he said no more. Right then, she wanted to go away somewhere where she knew no one. If she had a complete break, that might clear her head. Maybe she could go to Pinecraft and be near the water.

"What are you thinking, Rosie?"

"I'm thinking of going somewhere warm, near the water."

"On a vacation?"

"*Jah*, I think I need one, away by myself somewhere."

"Why don't you ask the bishop if he can arrange for you to stay with someone somewhere? He knows lots of people."

"You know, I just might."

They were interrupted by a group of people who wanted Mark's opinion on something. Rose wasn't included in the conversation so she gradually backed away.

Several minutes later, she was talking to the twins telling them they had to leave soon, when Mark asked to speak with her again.

The twins giggled as their older sister walked away with Mark.

"What is it?" Rose asked when they were far enough away not to be overheard.

"I just wanted to make sure you're okay."

"I'm fine. I'm just nervous about going to the bishop's *haus* tomorrow. I mean, what do I say?"

"Just smile a lot and nod. Agree to pray about everything and ask the bishop some questions about the Bible. He loves to answer questions."

"Does he?"

"*Jah*, he'll forget about the reason you're there and start talking about the Scriptures."

"Really?"

Mark nodded. "Have a couple of questions ready."

Rose giggled. "I'll do that. *Denke*."

Chapter Twenty

The Lord is my strength and my shield; my heart trusted in him, and I am helped: therefore my heart greatly rejoiceth; and with my song will I praise him.

Psalm 28:7

When Rose was comfortably seated in the bishop's living room, Olga sat down beside Bishop John, and then he began, "Rose, you're here because your parents are concerned. There was a situation with Jacob Schumacher."

Rose looked at the bishop and then Olga wondering how much they'd heard. "Oh, that's all been resolved."

"They said you took it hard when he left with Jessica," the bishop said.

"Do you know Jessica?" Rose asked trying to deflect the comment.

Olga, interrupted, "We met Jessica and her aunt when they came here about Jacob and the dreadful, sinful situation they were in."

Rose wondered what Olga was talking about and then noticed that the bishop shot a look of disapproval toward his wife, as though she'd revealed information that was confidential. Sin? Had Jacob done something wrong?

Olga glanced at her husband who was still staring at her, and said, "I'll get us some hot tea."

"I'll help you," the bishop said. "I'll be back in a moment, Rose." Before he left the room, he turned back to Rose, and explained, "The pot is too heavy for Olga to lift once it's full."

"Okay."

Once Bishop John and Olga were in the kitchen, Rose decided she wanted coffee instead. She jumped up and walked to the kitchen door and found it closed. Then she didn't want to go in, in case they were talking about something private. She listened while she decided whether she should walk in or not.

She heard the bishop say, "Olga, you've got to keep things quiet about Jessica and Jacob. If anyone finds out that Jessica is expecting a *boppli* out of wedlock, things will be uncomfortable for them. Once they're married, no one needs be any the wiser."

Rose clapped her hand over her mouth in shock. That's why things had been so sudden. That's why the old lady with Jessica was so cross, and that explained why Jacob had gone back to Jessica.

Rose shook her head, feeling a little faint. She'd had a close call. If Jacob hadn't been taken away from her so quickly, she could've fallen victim to him just like Jessica had. He'd forced her to kiss him, and then he'd even hinted that more than kissing would be okay. It was odd, but Rose was relieved and grateful for the experience, as awful as it was. Jacob wasn't the man for her—not at all. But if she'd been wrong about Jacob, how could she trust her feelings again? He had made it all sound so right.

She heard the bishop's hushed voice once more. "Just be careful what you say," he said to Olga.

Rose scurried back to the couch and had just reached it when the kitchen door opened.

"Sorry to leave you alone like that, Rose."

"That's okay."

"Now, where were we?" the bishop asked.

Remembering what Mark told her, Rose asked, "I forget quite honestly, but I have a question about Moses."

He smiled and with a slight raise of his bushy black eyebrows, asked, "What is it?"

"How did he divide the Red Sea? I've always wondered. Did it really happen literally?"

"Ah, I'm glad you asked. It was a miracle. You see…"

Rose settled back in the couch and listened to the bishop talk about Moses and the crossing of the Red Sea on dry land.

While she watched the bishop's mouth open and close above his long bushy beard, she thought about Mark. He wasn't tall, he wasn't over-confident, but he was someone she could trust. Without a doubt, she knew she could trust him with everything she held dear. She didn't love Mark with her heart the way she'd loved Jacob, but then and there she decided she would open her mind and her heart to the possibility of love with Mark. If, of course, he still felt the same way about her after she'd paid him no mind for years.

Olga brought the tea out on a large tray and set it down on a table in front of Rose. "Here you go, dear."

"Denke." Rose leaned forward and picked up a teacup.

"Did I answer the question sufficiently, Rose? Do you understand all I said about Moses?"

"*Jah.* It was really interesting. I've wondered about all that for some time."

An hour later, Rose left the bishop's house and got into the buggy with her father.

"Did his talk help you?" he asked.

"It really did. You and *Mamm* were right to have me talk with him and Olga. I found out some things." Rose smiled. She found out some things because she'd overheard the truth about Jacob.

"*Gut!* Then, let's go home and tell your *mudder* you're feeling better."

Rose nodded.

With Mark's change of vocation, Rose had to wait until the next Sunday meeting before she saw him again. When she sat with Tulip at the back of the room, she watched Mark enter the house and sit down with his younger brother.

There was a different feeling when she saw him, she was certain about it. She probably just missed seeing him every day.

Tulip leaned over closer to her, and whispered, "Just because things ended badly with Jacob, don't rebound onto Mark. I've noticed people do things like that and it's not good. Be sure about who you want first."

Rose stared at Tulip. Tulip must've seen her looking at Mark, and somehow guessed that Rose was thinking of him as a possible boyfriend. Was she rebounding, though? She'd never considered Mark as a serious marriage partner before this, so why now? "I'm not sure how I feel."

"That's why you should wait. Don't rush into things. You gave your heart too early to Jacob and look how that ended. There's plenty of time. It's not a race."

Rose nodded. Tulip had a good point. She should keep her distance from Mark and then wait to see what happened. She leaned over to her sister. "*Mamm's* the one who doesn't want me to wait. She's putting pressure on me to marry, saying she'll give me a year."

"I think she feels different now, since things happened the way they did with Jacob."

Rose was relieved and only hoped that were true. "Are you sure?"

"*Jah*, she was talking about it yesterday."

"Not in front of the twins I hope."

"*Nee*, just with me," Tulip said.

"What did she say exactly?"

"Just that she blames herself for the whole Jacob thing."

Rose frowned. "It's not her fault."

"I tried to tell her that. It was Jacob's fault."

The deacon, Rose's father, stood before the congregation and said a prayer. Rose and Tulip could no longer whisper in the back row or he'd see them. It saddened Rose to learn that her mother blamed herself for what had happened.

After the meeting, Rose sat alone by a tree feeling sorry for herself. She hadn't even noticed anyone approach.

"Why so gloomy?"

She looked up to see Mark, and then she forced a laugh. "I don't know. I'm just thinking about some things."

He stood next to her. "Mind if I sit?"

"Would it matter?"

"It would."

She nodded. "You can sit down."

"Mighty nice of you." He sat beside her on the wooden log seat.

Rose smiled and gazed into the distance.

"Does this gloominess have anything to do with Jacob?"

She nodded. "I made a fool of myself."

"You didn't."

"I feel like I have and everyone probably knows about it by now. News travels fast."

"It's plain to see that you were…fond of him, I'll say that."

She shook her head and shuddered. "That was a big mistake."

"The mistake was his and he made it before he met you, Rosie."

She whipped her head around to look at him. "You know?"

"There's not much that escapes me. I might act dopey, but it's just an act. I'm actually a genius. Too many people would become jealous if they knew the truth about the power of my brain." He looked from side to side as though he was worried that someone might be listening.

Rose couldn't help but laugh at him. He always made her feel better. If only she could still see him every day.

"What I'm hoping is that I can take advantage of someone else's mistake," Mark said.

"That sounds ruthless."

"I'm a ruthless genius."

"And how would you go about taking advantage of someone's mistake anyway?"

"That's my secret."

"You can't tell me something like that, Mark, and not follow through with an explanation."

He sighed. "It's pretty clear, Rosie. Jacob has to marry

someone else other than you. How would I turn that to my advantage?" He stared at her with such intensity that she had to look away. He still liked her just as she hoped and he hadn't been put off by her liking Jacob.

Mark continued, "I've always felt a certain way toward you, and I've always hoped that you might feel the same way about me. I love you, Rosie."

She turned her head around once more to look into his eyes. "You do?"

He nodded.

"Why did you encourage me with Jacob? Why did you ask me to have dinner at your *haus* when he was there?"

He shrugged his shoulders. "I've just been hanging around hoping you'd feel the same one day. There are only so many hints I can drop. All those jokes and whatnot that I say to you—I mean them. I've always meant them. I've always hoped you'll marry me and perhaps one day see something in me that you've never seen before. That's my hope anyway."

Rose looked down. Her heart was bruised and not ready to let anyone else in.

"You don't have to say anything, Rosie. I'll have to settle for your friendship if that's all you have to offer. I need you in my life and if it'll only ever be that you and I stay friends then I'll consider myself a man most blessed. Blessed because…" He put his hand on his heart. "You are… I can't find words. You are just *wunderbaar!*"

She laughed. No one had ever talked that way about her before. With Jacob it had all been lies and it somehow felt as though he was always out of reach. Here was Mark who had all the goodness, principles, and kindness that she'd always wanted in a man, but did she love him? There were no butterflies in her tummy.

Amish Rose

"I don't know what to say, Mark."

He shook his head slightly smiling at her. "You don't need to say anything, but I need to ask you something."

She gulped. "What?"

"Rosie, will you marry me?"

She gulped again. "I don't know…it's too soon because…"

"Don't say anything more. I didn't think you would. I just wanted to let you know in all honesty how much I would love you to be my *fraa.*" He stood up. "I'll never be far away, Rosie, if you ever change your mind."

Rose sat there and watched him walk away. Part of her wanted to run after him, but there was another part that told her Mark wasn't her perfect man. He wasn't the one she'd always imagined. Tulip had been right to caution her. Just because Jacob had been a disaster, she shouldn't settle for someone who was nice and wouldn't break her heart. Someone else might come along who suited her better than Mark and be more like the dream man she'd always imagined.

Chapter Twenty-One

Delight thyself also in the Lord: and he shall give thee the desires of thine heart. Commit thy way unto the Lord; trust also in him; and he shall bring it to pass.

Psalm 37:4-5

A whole year passed. Months ago, Rose had held her oldest brother's newborn baby in her arms, and she desperately wanted to have a baby of her own. Some weeks after that, she heard whispers that a child had been born to Jessica and Jacob. Of course, the child had been born less than nine months after their marriage, but that was swept under the rug and not mentioned. Still, the news of the birth reminded Rose of how she'd been fooled by Jacob and it sent her into a dark depression.

Nancy Yoder sat her oldest daughter down one Monday morning before Rose left for work.

"Rose, it's been more than a year now since I spoke to you about you getting married. You haven't been out with anyone since Jacob. Your *vadder* told me to let you be, but what's going on? There are ten weddings booked now in the time since Jacob left. One of those weddings should've been yours."

"I told you, *Mamm*, getting married is something I won't do until I find someone who suits me. I won't be forced into something just for the sake of it."

"There are a dozen men, any of which would suit you. What are you waiting, or looking, for? It's not setting a good example for your sisters. They seem just as uninterested in the whole idea of marriage as you are and I can only blame you for that."

Rose tugged at the strings of her prayer *kapp*. "I don't know."

"You don't know about what?" Her mother was using her angry voice.

"Anything, really… I guess."

"Well, perhaps that's where we should start. We shall work out what problem you have with marriage and clear it up. Perhaps another talk with the bishop would be in order?"

"*Nee*, not the bishop again, please, *Mamm*."

"Okay, but you can't escape talking with me. Tonight's the night, right after dinner."

Rose stood up. "Okay tonight it is, but right now I need to go to work. Mrs. Walker needs me to start a little earlier today. She'll be here soon. They're redoing the roof over the market and we might need to move the stall to the other end for a few days. The managers are letting us know today."

"Okay, Rose, but we will speak tonight. And we'll put a plan into place. You're making too big a thing out of this. One man is as *gut* as another."

"Really?" Rose raised her eyebrows. "I wonder what *Dat* would think about that?"

Mrs. Yoder giggled and wagged her finger at her daughter. "I didn't mean it like that."

Rose smiled and then leaned over and kissed her mother on her cheek. "I'll see you later, *Mamm*."

"Don't forget we need to talk tonight."

"There's no danger of that. You've talked about nothing else these last few minutes."

Rose hurried down the driveway to meet Mrs. Walker. She'd long since gotten over Jacob and the hurt he'd caused her heart. Jacob hadn't been respectful toward her and now that more time had passed, she could see that clearly. She felt sorry for Jessica, the girl he'd married.

Mark and she hadn't been as close as they once were. It was kind of awkward between them ever since Mark had asked her to marry him. She'd thought about Mark and his proposal every single day. She couldn't find a reason not to accept his proposal except for a nagging doubt. After months of self-examination, Rose realized that her doubt was purely based on the fact that she'd always seen herself with someone different from Mark. She was a tall girl and Mark was barely a shade taller and she'd always imagined herself married to someone so much taller, as tall as Jacob. Besides that, Mark was easily available to her and there was something within her that wanted the excitement of the exotic stranger, someone new and exciting—as Jacob had been.

Is it that simple? She slowed down when she nearly reached the road. Looking down she kicked the pebbles along the driveway. Rose missed talking and laughing with Mark every day. What if he no longer wanted her? Could he have grown tired of waiting? She knew he wasn't dating anyone—she hadn't heard he was, at least.

She leaned against the gatepost at the end of the drive,

waiting for Mrs. Walker while she thought about men. Her relationship with Jacob had been exciting, but it had also caused her pain. Jacob wasn't honest and forthright, whereas Mark had told her exactly how he felt about her and that had taken great courage. Rose could appreciate that now that time had passed.

Maybe she loved Mark. Or was it love? Could it be love or simply that there was no one else around? Was that why she now felt as though she might love him?

She heaved a loud sigh. *This is all too confusing!*

When she heard the *clip-clopping* of hooves, she looked up to see Mrs. Walker's gray horse pulling the buggy.

When they arrived at the markets, Rose found out that the Walkers had to move their stall to the other side while the roof was being repaired. That also meant that Rose wouldn't be next to Mark's younger brother and the goat-cheese stall.

When the midday rush was over, she looked up and saw Mark walking toward her. Her heart pounded in her ears while at the same time she hoped she looked all right.

"Hi, Mark, it's nice to see you."

"Hello, Rosie, I've come to check on Matthew."

"They've had to move us all around."

"I know. I hope it won't be for too long. Our regular customers mightn't be able to find us."

"You're not working today?" Rose asked.

He laughed. "I've got the day off. It's the advantage of *not* working in the *familye* business. Goats have to be milked every day."

"That sounds *gut*, that you can have a day off."

She stared at him. Had he grown a little taller and

was he a little heavier? He looked more of a man now rather than a teenager. How great a difference a year had made. Sure she'd seen him every couple of weeks at the meetings, but she'd never really 'looked' at him like she was now.

"How have you been, Rosie?"

She desperately wanted to tell him that she'd missed him. She swallowed hard against the lump that had formed in her throat. "I've been okay."

"You look lovely."

Rose giggled. *"Denke."*

"Well, I'd better have a look to see where our stall's been placed."

"I'm sure it's over that way." She pointed to the western corner of the building.

"I'll come back and talk after I see Matthew."

Rose nodded. "I'd like that."

She watched him walk away and to her surprise she was tingling, and she could only put that down to being nervous.

A loud boom shook the ground underneath her and Rose grabbed hold of the table in front of her. The roof that was being fixed had collapsed, and billows of dust filled the air. Her stall was outside under an annex and had escaped the disaster. Everything took place in slow motion, as though she were in a dream. There was an eerie silence and then all at once screams and cries rang through the air. Seconds later, Rose stood stunned as people ran to and fro.

Chapter Twenty-Two

Now faith is the substance of things hoped for, the evidence of things not seen.

Hebrews 11:1

"Mark!" Rose screamed as she ran toward the rubble.

Suddenly Mark appeared amongst the dust and debris. He yelled for someone to call Emergency Services. Then he organized men in the crowd that had gathered, forming teams to start moving the rubble aside to get people out.

When Mark saw Rose, he yelled at her to stay back.

All Rose could do was stand there and watch the scene unfold as though it wasn't really happening. It was too awful to be true. Mark could've been killed, and where was Matthew? Rose knew Matthew was somewhere under the pile of wooden beams and roofing fragments with many of the other workers.

Soon Mark and the men he'd organized were pulling out the wounded. A sense of relief came at the sound of the sirens of the police, fire and paramedic vehicles.

Rose closed her eyes tightly and prayed that Matthew was somewhere safe where he wasn't harmed. When

Rose opened her eyes, she saw an upright beam tilt, and Mark was directly underneath it. She screamed and ran to him, but she was too late. He was lying there, still and motionless.

"Mark." She picked up his hand. The lower half of his body was trapped.

A pair of strong arms lifted her up and away. She turned to see a fireman.

"Stay clear, Ma'am."

"Help him!" Rose screamed pointing to Mark. Rose stayed on the side and watched as three firemen levered the wooden beam off him. Once it was off, the paramedics were called over to tend to him.

"Is he okay?" Rose leaned over and asked them.

"He's alive."

Rose looked around and couldn't see Matthew. She knew that would be Mark's first concern. "His brother's still in there somewhere."

"They're doing all they can to get everyone out. Stand back, Ma'am. We're ready to move him." The paramedics moved Mark onto a stretcher and Rose ran alongside until they put him in an ambulance.

"Are you his wife?" one of them asked as he closed the double doors at the rear of the vehicle.

"No, I'm just a friend." Thinking it didn't reflect their relationship, she added, "A really good friend."

After the paramedic had told Rose which hospital he'd be taken to, Rose ran back to look for Matthew. To her relief, she found Matthew sitting with people who were waiting for medical attention.

She silently thanked God that he was still alive. "Matthew, are you okay?"

"*Jah*, Rose, nothing major. How are you?"

"I'm okay, but they've just taken Mark to the hos-

pital. A huge wooden beam fell on him and he's been
knocked out."

Matthew's bottom lip trembled. "Mark was here?"

"*Jah.* He came to see where your stall had been
placed. I've got to go to him to make sure he'll be fine.
I mean, I'm sure he is. He's in good hands. Are you sure
you're okay?"

Matthew gulped and nodded. "I'm just a bit dizzy.
Go and be with him please, Rose. He'll want you to be
with him."

Rose nodded and ran to grab her belongings from behind the flower stall. At least that had escaped the damage. Then she headed out to the main road to catch a taxi.

Rose was relieved when she arrived at the hospital.
She was told that Mark had regained consciousness; he
had a slight concussion and a broken leg.

He was still in the emergency section and she was
shown to his bedside where a nurse was adjusting his
drip.

"What are you doing here?" His eyes were half open
and his speech was slurred.

"I'm here to make certain you'll be okay." She grabbed
his hand.

"I'm fine, but I can't marry you."

A nurse was adjusting his IV drip, and whispered to
Rose, "It's the drugs talking."

Rose nodded and smoothed back Mark's hair, careful
of the bandage on his head. "You can't?"

"*Nee*, I can't. I can't marry you in here."

"The doctor will be back to see him soon." The nurse
shot Rose a big smile before she made her way through
the curtains that separated Mark from the other patients
in Emergency.

"But you still want to marry me?" Rose asked Mark.

He smiled back. "Nothing I'd like better," he whispered before his eyes gradually closed.

Rose leaned closer to check that he was still breathing. What part of his words were his and what part was the pain medication? Would he still want to marry her after so long? She looked down at their hands clasped together and tears fell down her face. As long as he got healthy again, that's all that mattered.

Suddenly the curtains were pulled aside. A man in a white coat stepped through and introduced himself as a doctor.

"Will he be okay?" Rose asked.

"Are you a relative?"

"No." She then realized she should've called Mark's parents.

The doctor glanced down at their clasped hands.

"We're engaged," she announced.

"Congratulations!" The doctor smiled and then told her about Mark's injuries and what he expected of his recovery. "He'll sleep now. He's had strong medication and you won't get any sense out of him. He'll be out of Emergency and in a ward tomorrow if you want to come back in the morning."

Rose nodded. "Is it okay if I sit with him for a while?"

"Of course, but he won't know you're here."

Rose stayed by his side another hour before she thought about her family and the Walker family. They would've heard about the disaster by now and would be wondering where she was. She leaned over and left a soft kiss on Mark's forehead. Before she left the hospital, her first call was to Mark and Matthew's mother to tell her what had happened and where her sons were.

* * *

When the taxi stopped at Rose's house, her mother rushed out the front door.

"Rose, you're okay."

Rose finished paying the driver and quickly got out of the car because she knew how her mother was prone to panicking at the slightest thing. *"Jah, Mamm."* Rose repeated everything she told her on the phone. "I'm okay. I just had to leave the stall because there was so much devastation everywhere. Mark is in the hospital with a broken leg and concussion and Matthew has got something wrong with him but he's not too bad. The paramedics were looking after him when I left for the hospital to see how Mark was."

Her mother wrapped her arms around her. "I'm so grateful you're okay."

As they walked to the house, Tulip ran out and she was promptly instructed by their mother to call the Walkers to tell them Rose was fine.

"I had to leave the flowers," Rose said as Tulip hurried to the phone in the barn.

"I've had Mrs. Walker over here and she told me everything that happened. She was very worried about you because no one knew where you were."

Rose bit her lip and stopped still at the bottom of the porch steps. "I don't know why I didn't call her. I thought of it, but everything was happening so fast. I called Mrs. Schumacher and told her where Matthew and Mark were."

"That would've been a hard call to make. Come inside now. You look all pale, much paler than usual. You need something to eat and drink."

That was the last thing Rose felt like, but she didn't

have enough energy to argue with her mother after all that had happened.

As soon as she stepped into the house, she was faced with the twins who rapidly asked her questions one after the other. Rose answered as many of them as she could. "As far as I know, no one died, but many were injured."

Their mother ordered, "Stop asking so many things. Daisy, make her a cup of tea."

"Okay," Daisy said.

"It's okay, *Mamm*, I don't mind answering questions."

"What would you like to eat?" Lily asked.

"Would you like to eat in the kitchen or the living room?" Daisy asked.

Rose was touched that her twin sisters were being so nice to her. They usually kept to themselves. "In the kitchen is fine, *denke*."

"Mrs. Walker said that she's glad you're okay and they're heading into the markets to see what's left of their stall."

"*Denke* for calling her, Tulip," Rose said. "Their stall's okay. It wasn't in the badly damaged area."

They sat in the kitchen, the four girls and their mother, while Rose told them all about the horrible event she had witnessed. "And you should have seen the way Mark took charge before the paramedics and emergency team got there. It was as though he was somebody else."

"I wonder if that will be in the papers tomorrow," Daisy said.

"Of course it would be," their mother said. "Things like that are always in the papers."

Lily said, "I wonder if they will have something about Mark in the paper if he was such a hero like Rose said."

"Are you doubting what Rose said, really?" Tulip asked.

"*Nee*, not so much. It's just that she likes Mark, so she thinks anything he does is spectacular. I was wondering what other people thought, that's all."

Their mother shook her head. "I'm sure Rose wasn't making anything up."

"I didn't say she was, *Mamm*." Lily heaved a sigh. "Why does this always happen? Everyone in this family always takes everything I say the wrong way."

"I don't," said Daisy.

"I didn't mean you, everyone except you turns everything around to make me look like I'm the bad one."

"I know what you mean," Daisy said nodding.

"You two always stick up for each other," Tulip said. "Anyway, I don't know why everything has to turn into an argument. Mark did a good thing in helping people and what does it matter if no one else noticed that apart from Rose?"

Rose remained silent as she hugged her warm teacup with both hands.

"Rose is in love with Mark," Lily said.

"Everyone knows that," Daisy added with a high-pitched giggle.

"Come on, girls, Rose doesn't need this right now. Up to your rooms the both of you."

The twins looked at each other with pouting faces.

Daisy asked, "Can we go to the same room?"

Their mother sighed. "*Jah*, do what you want as long as it's upstairs and you leave Rose alone for the rest of the night."

"How long do we have to stay in our rooms?" Lily asked.

"Until morning."

"Come on, Lily, there's no use arguing. They don't

think we're adults." Daisy stood up and grabbed Lily's arm.

Their mother narrowed her eyes. "When you behave like adults, I'll treat you like adults."

The twins left the room and Rose took another sip of tea.

Her mother put a hand on Rose's arm. "I'm so glad you're unharmed."

"Me too," Tulip added.

"It was so dreadful. I don't know how it happened. I'm just glad no one was killed. I hope no one was killed. Unless they found someone after I left." Rose put her tea-cup on the table and covered her face with both hands. "It was awful. And it was horrible to see Mark lying in the hospital."

"How is he?" Tulip asked.

"Broken leg and concussion. They said I can go see him tomorrow morning and he might be able to talk. He barely said two words to me and what he said didn't make much sense."

"Lie down on the couch and have a rest, Rose."

"Okay." The couch in the living room was where the girls went when they didn't feel well but weren't really ill. It was comforting to sit by the fire on the soft couch looking out the large window at the trees and the distant fields.

That night Rose lay in bed worrying. Had she missed her chance with Mark by foolishly choosing his cousin a year ago? It was an embarrassing mistake, which thankfully not many people knew about. Her door opened slightly and she saw Tulip's silhouette at the door. "Come in."

"I didn't know whether you'd still be awake." Tulip

came further into her room and sat down on her bed while Rose pushed herself up into a seated position.

"I have so many things going around in my head."

"I thought you would. You still like Mark, don't you?"

"I do, but it's a different thing that I feel. I don't want to be without Mark in my life and I want to see him every day. I didn't think he gave me butterflies, but when I saw him yesterday, I felt something in my tummy."

"Was that before or after he was saving everybody?"

Rose smiled. "That was before. Helping everyone like that showed what type of man he is."

"He's a brave man and a man of action."

Rose nodded. "*Jah*, he's a real man and that's what I want."

"Mmm. That's very attractive in a man."

"Tulip, what if he had died yesterday? I mean today. It's still today, isn't it?"

"*Jah*, it's still today. It's only about eleven o'clock."

"He could've died and then I would've regretted things. He was always asking me to marry him but what about now? Does he still want me after all this time?"

"That's something you'll have to find out from him."

Rose put a hand over her stomach. "I hope I haven't left things too late."

"I don't think you have. He's always liked you."

Rose nibbled on the end of her fingernail. "I'll have to call the Walkers tomorrow to see what's happening with the stall. I guess I won't be working again for a while. I don't know what will happen."

"I guess so. They'll probably shut the markets down for repair."

"I'll go to the hospital first thing and see him," Rose said.

"Good idea."

* * *

The next morning, knowing that he would be out of the emergency, Rose found out from the reception desk that Mark was in room 209. She hurried to the second floor and when she walked into his room, she saw four occupied beds and then she saw two Amish women talking to the person in the far bed.

Taking a step closer, she recognized the back of the young women. They were Lucy Stoltzfuz and Becky Miller. Rose had grown up with them and so too had Mark.

The two young women turned around and greeted her. She gave a quick nod and then focused her attention on Mark, who looked pale, but was smiling.

"Rose, you came back."

"You remember I was here yesterday?"

"Of course I do."

Lucy said, "It's all over the papers what happened at the markets and they're calling Mark a local hero."

"Really? I wondered if it was going to be in the papers."

"Did you really save all those people?" Becky asked him.

"*Nee.* I didn't save anyone. That's what the paramedics did. I didn't do much at all."

"That's not what everyone's saying." Lucy's face beamed.

Mark gave a low chuckle. "I can't help what others say."

"Has the doctor been to see you this morning?" Rose asked.

"Not yet, but no doubt I'll see him sometime today."

"How did you hear about Mark being in the hospital?" Rose asked the two young women.

"My mother heard it from someone," Lucy said. "They said that the roof in the farmers market had collapsed, Mark and Matthew were injured and Mark was in the hospital. We had to come and see how he was."

"You can see I'm perfectly fine. No need for anybody to worry."

Becky sat on his bed and grabbed hold of his hand. "Oh, Mark, I don't know what I would've done if something bad had happened to you."

"Me either," Lucy said.

Rose could tell that Mark was lapping up all the attention. She never realized that Lucy or Becky were that close to him and that was because she hadn't had much to do with him over the past year. Perhaps the article in the paper made them look at him in a different light. It was uncomfortable watching the two women throw themselves at him.

Rose waited for a break in the conversation, and then said, "I might come back a little later."

"You could come back at visiting hours, Rose," Becky said.

"*Jah*, we just sneaked in," Lucy said.

Becky added, "Because visiting hours aren't until later. Ten to twelve in the morning and then between one and three in the afternoon."

Rose nodded. "I'll be back soon, Mark." She smiled at Mark and said goodbye to the two women before she left the room. Mark hadn't even urged her to stay and she took that as a bad sign. She was only going to wait half an hour or so in the hospital cafeteria until they left so she could talk to Mark alone, but he hadn't known that.

He seemed happy enough with the company of the two women. For all he knew, she could've been heading home and not coming back until the next day.

When Rose found the cafeteria, she slumped into one of the chairs at one of the several round tables. There she wondered what to do. Then she decided if Mark wanted one of those women over her, there was nothing she could do about it. She was the one who didn't know what she had until she'd lost it and she couldn't blame Mark for that. He'd waited for her for a long time without her giving him an ounce of encouragement. And how would he have felt several months ago when he found out she'd liked Jacob? She put her elbows on the table and held her head in both hands.

"Are you alright, dear?" An old lady had sat down beside her and she hadn't even noticed.

"Oh, yes, I'm okay."

"Do you have a loved one in the hospital?"

She stared into the old woman's face and noticed how her beady blue eyes studied her. "I do, but he's not seriously ill. He's got a concussion and a broken leg, so he'll live."

"That is good news."

Rose took her elbows off the table and straightened her back. "Yes, it is. You're right. It is good news."

"I thought you had lost somebody."

Rose smiled at the kindly woman. "I haven't. Not yet."

The old lady smiled back and then turned her attention to her teacup, ripped open a packet of sugar and poured it into her tea.

Rose went to the counter and ordered a coffee. Once she finished drinking her coffee, she planned to go back to Mark. Hopefully by then, his admirers would've left.

Rose put her head around Mark's door and saw that Lucy and Becky had gone. She was instantly relieved and was just about to walk into the room when she heard a voice behind her.

"I'm sorry, but it's not visiting hours yet."

Rose swung around and in front of her was one of the blue uniformed hospital staff. "I'm sorry. I didn't know there were particular visiting hours until I got here. Can I just say a quick hello?"

The female worker frowned at her.

"Please? I won't be long and then I'll go."

The worker gave a curt nod and walked away.

Rose wasted no time in hurrying to see Mark. His face lit up when he noticed her walking toward him. "Rosie, you're back."

She liked him calling her Rosie; it was just like old times.

"There were too many people here before, so I thought I'd wait until they were gone."

"*Denke* for coming."

"Why wouldn't I visit you?"

"I didn't mean it like that. I'm glad that you did, that's all. Come closer and sit on the bed."

She glanced over her shoulder, and then said, "I just got into trouble for being here out of visiting hours, so I can't stay long."

"Just a moment longer."

She sat on the edge of his bed pleased that he was so happy to see her.

"You're looking good today. I was worried about you yesterday."

"I'm feeling a lot better. The nurse said I'd feel tingling or itching on my leg as the drugs wear off."

"How long do they think you'll be in here?"

"I guess that's up to the doctor whenever he gets here."

"I didn't know you were particularly friends with Becky and Lucy."

"A lot has changed in the last year, Rosie."

Rose would've asked more questions but considering the state of his health they were questions best left for another day. "Can I bring you anything while you're in here?"

"*Nee, denke.* There's nothing I need except to see your friendly face. You'll come back and see me again, won't you?"

Those words pleased her immensely. "I will. I'll be back to see you every day. Have your parents been here yet?"

"They were here last night and they said they were coming back this afternoon. Matthew just had cuts and bruises; nothing serious."

"That's good. I was wondering about that." She looked over her shoulder at the door hoping that the person who told her about the visiting hours wasn't going to come back and check on her. It was then that she noticed the people in the other beds. Two of them were old men who were asleep, the other one was a young man watching the television with earphones in his ears. "I should go before they kick me out."

"You'll come back tomorrow?" he asked again.

"I will. I don't think that the Walkers can have their flower stall at the markets now. I'm not sure what's going to happen. Either way, I'll get here and see you tomorrow."

His eyes started closing. "I'll see you tomorrow, Rosie."

She got off the bed. "Bye, Mark."

"Bye, Rosie."

She turned and headed out the door. Before she got to

the end of the corridor, Mark's doctor stepped out of the last door. They made eye-contact and the doctor stopped and smiled at her. "Mark's fiancée?"

"Yes. You have a good memory."

He chuckled. "We don't get that many Amish people in here."

"I've just been to see him. He seems a lot better. When do you think he'll be able to go home?"

"Perhaps tomorrow or the day after."

"That soon?"

"Most likely the day after. It depends on his progress."

"I see. Thank you, doctor." Rose hurried away glad that nobody heard him calling her Mark's fiancée. She probably shouldn't have told him that, but she couldn't go back in time and change things.

Rose took a taxi directly to Mrs. Walker's house to find out what was going on with the flower stall. The damage caused from the collapse of the roof would take weeks and maybe even months to repair.

The Walkers had made the decision to set up a roadside stall. The market stall was only a small part of their business and their only retail outlet of their large wholesale flower business. They wouldn't suffer too much financially from what happened, but that wasn't the case for the Schumachers. The bulk of their goats' milk products were through the market stall and they would need to find another outlet to sell their goods.

Rose walked home from the Walkers'. Even though they lived on the next-door property, they weren't close enough to be able to see the Walkers' home from their house. Only the rows of temperature-controlled greenhouses could be seen.

As soon as Rose opened her front door, her mother rushed toward her followed close by the twins, and then Tulip.

"How is he?" her mother asked.

"He's fine and he'll need to stay in for a couple more days. That's what the doctor said."

"That's good and have you heard how Matthew is?"

"Just scrapes and some bruises. He's fine. Mark was in the papers and they called him a hero."

"Who was in the papers?" Daisy asked. "Mark was in the papers?"

"*Jah*, he was."

"I said he was going to be," Lily said.

Daisy stuck her chin out. "*Nee*, I said it."

"Quiet, girls," their mother said. "It doesn't matter who said it." She looked at Rose. "Did you get one of the newspapers?"

"I didn't think to get it."

"Why not?"

"*Dat* doesn't like the *Englisch* papers." Rose hoped her mother wouldn't send her back out to get a paper. She was too tired to go anywhere.

"It wouldn't hurt to just get one to see what they said about Mark."

"Rose, why don't you and I go out and get one now?"

Rose looked at Tulip. Even though she was weary, getting out of the house and being with Tulip sounded like a good idea. "*Jah*, why don't we do that? Is that okay with you, *Mamm*?"

"*Jah*, go on."

"Let's go, Rose." Tulip stepped forward and grabbed Rose's arm and pulled her back toward the front door.

The two girls set about hitching the buggy.

"What happened at the hospital? It's like something's bothering you."

"You can tell?" Rose asked.

"It's written all over your face. I'm surprised *Mamm* couldn't tell."

Rose rubbed her forehead. "When I got there, to Mark's hospital room, Lucy and Becky were there."

"Do you think one of them likes him?"

Rose nodded. "Or both of them do because that's how they were acting. They were telling Mark how brave he was and what a hero he was, and all that. And then one of them grabbed his hand. I can't remember which one it was. At that point, I left. I went and had a cup of coffee and waited for them to leave. Then I went back again."

"Had they left when you went back?"

"*Jah*, but I couldn't stay long because it wasn't visiting hours."

"Do you think Mark likes one of them?"

"It's hard to say. He didn't look upset to have them there, put it that way."

"He couldn't though, because that would've been rude. He would've liked to have visitors no matter who they were. Besides that, he probably sees them as just friends."

Rose nibbled on a fingernail. "Do you think that's just it? Do you think they're just friends?"

"I don't know. I haven't noticed them talking to him at the meetings or anything. How would we find out?"

"I suppose we could ask around, but that would be a little nosey and I wouldn't like to do that."

While Tulip backed the horse into the harness, she said, "So, we just wait and see how things unfold?"

"I guess that's what we do." When the horse was

hitched to the buggy, Rose patted him on his neck. "I said I'd go back and see him tomorrow."

"Do you want me to go too? That way, if he has visitors besides you, I can talk to them while you talk with Mark."

"*Denke.* That's a *gut* idea."

When Rose and Tulip got to the small supermarket that sold the daily newspapers, they saw that the news about the farmers market had made the front page. Tulip grabbed the paper and scanned the article while Rose looked for Mark's name over Tulip's shoulder.

"It says here a local Amish man, Mark Schumacher, pulled people from the rubble and took charge until the paramedics arrived."

"That's pretty much how it happened," Rose said.

Tulip took the paper to the counter to pay for it and then they headed back to the buggy. "Rose, if you want Mark, I think you have to move fast because women would want a man like Mark—a man who would put others before himself and risk his life to help others. There's something very attractive about a man who would do that."

Rose could barely speak and she hoped she hadn't left things too long. She'd only just realized how she felt, and now she would have to compete with other women for his attention. A year ago, no one gave him a second look or a second thought, including her.

"Well, what do you think?" Tulip asked as they both climbed into the buggy.

"You're right. I don't know what to do. I've got to sort my feelings out first."

"I think you know your feelings and you don't want to admit them to yourself."

Tulip moved the horse forward.

"That doesn't make much sense."

"It does. It makes perfect sense. You've always been in love with Mark and you didn't know it. You expected love to be something else."

Tulip was right in a sense. Rose thought back to Jacob. He was tall and handsome and had a dazzling smile and he'd said all the right things, but it was deep inside a man that mattered. Jacob wasn't half the man Mark was. She knew that if she married Mark he would always put her first and look after her.

"Why have you gone quiet, Rose?"

"I'm thinking about Jacob and how he made my heart pound. The first time I saw him I was sure we would be married."

"It wasn't real though. He's more handsome than Mark and probably more handsome then most men, but he's too in love with himself to ever be in love with a woman. That's what I reckon. You can easily do without Jacob, but can you do without Mark in your life?"

"I've really missed him over this past year. I always thought of him as a friend until he wasn't there."

"And that's when you started to think of him as something else?"

Rose covered her face with her hands. "I'm so confused."

"There's nothing confusing about it. Either you love him, or you don't. And if you don't, you must release him from your heart and your mind, so some other woman can have him and make him happy."

Rose was a little embarrassed to admit to her sister that she loved Mark because if she said it out loud she would feel bad about not realizing it earlier. "I wonder what *Dat* will say when he sees the thing about Mark in the paper?"

"He'll be pleased, of course."

When they got home, their mother told Rose that Mrs. Walker had stopped by to let Rose know that, along with other stallholders, they'd set up shop down the road from the markets. Rose was selfishly disappointed because it meant she wouldn't be free to visit Mark.

"I can work on the stall instead of you for a few days if you like, Rose."

"Would you?"

Tulip nodded. "I don't mind at all."

Rose looked back at her mother. "When are they going to start?"

"The day after tomorrow."

"Perfect. I'll walk over and talk to Mrs. Walker now and tell her that Tulip will do a couple of days for me." Rose knew she wouldn't mind. Tulip often filled in for her at the flower stall.

The next day, Tulip and Rose walked into Mark's hospital room at the start of visiting hours, and to Rose's delight, they were the only visitors.

Mark turned to look at them and smiled as they walked over. "I've got two visitors today. I can't pull any chairs closer for you. They tell me I can't walk just yet."

"It looks like it'll be sometime before you can," Tulip said while Rose pulled the two chairs by the wall close to his bed.

"It's not a bad break. The doctor just wanted to keep me in here because of the concussion. I feel fine. What's going on with you two?"

They sat down and Rose was the one who answered. "Tomorrow the Walkers are setting up a stall for their

flowers not far from the markets with a few stallholders. Are your parents doing the same?"

"I'm not certain. Our generator was destroyed and
now we're borrowing one and setting up somewhere.
My folks didn't say where."

"It's a shame about the generator being destroyed.
One that size would cost a lot of money."

"It did."

While Rose listened to Mark talk, she was pleased
that there was no sign of Becky or Lucy. "Have you been
getting many visitors?"

"Quite a few. The bishop and his wife came yesterday
afternoon along with a couple of my brothers."

"Tulip is looking after the stall for me, so I can come
back and see you tomorrow."

"That's very nice of you, Tulip. *Denke.*"

"I know how worried Rose has been about you."

Mark smiled at Rose. "I'm fine, Rosie, you don't need
to worry."

"I know, but it's hard to see you in the hospital like
this so helpless."

His lips turn down at the corners. "I'm not that helpless. They showed me how to walk on the crutches this
morning. A broken leg won't hold me back too much. It
could've been worse."

"Don't talk about it," Rose said. "It was very dangerous you going back into the building like that."

"If I remember correctly, I was out of the building
when something fell on me."

Tulip stood. "I'm going to get a soda. Can I bring you
back anything, Mark? Tea or coffee?"

"I'd love a strong coffee."

"Coming up. And you, Rose?"

"Nothing for me, *denke.*" Tulip walked out of the

room and Rose was pleased to be alone with Mark—
alone apart from the three other patients in the room.
None of them were listening. One had his earphones in
again, one was reading a book, and the other was asleep.

"I'll be out of here tomorrow or the next day. Most
likely tomorrow."

"That's good. They seem to be looking after you in
here."

"Yeah, they are, but I'd much rather be at home.
Denke for coming to see me again. I was hoping you
would."

Heat rose to her cheeks. She'd never been embarrassed or shy in front of him before. Now things were
different. Now that Tulip was out of the room and she
was alone with him, she desperately wanted him to know
that she liked him. He wasn't joking about marrying her
like he used to when they'd worked side-by-side at the
markets. "What about your job? Will you still be able
to make the buggies with a broken leg?"

"I'll be able to do some parts of my job. I'll work
around things somehow."

"That's good." When Rose heard loud voices in the
corridor, she recognized them as belonging to the two
girls who had visited him the other day. Her heart sank.
"It sounds like you have some more visitors heading
your way."

"*Jah*, their voices are unmistakable, aren't they?"

"I'll leave you alone with them and find Tulip."

"Will you come back?"

"*Jah*, we'll have to come back to give you your coffee."

"That's right. I'll see you soon then." As she was
about to leave, he lunged forward and grabbed her hand.

Then he whispered, "Don't leave me alone with them for too long."

Rose giggled. "I won't. We'll be back soon."

That confirmed to Rose that he didn't like either of them. He still liked her, she was sure of it. He let go of her hand when the two girls walked through the door.

"Rose, you're here again!" Lucy walked through the door followed closely by Becky.

"I am. I'm just leaving."

"Bye, Rose," Becky said as Rose walked past them.

It didn't sit well with Rose that they were visiting Mark again. She tried her best not to let it bother her. Just as she was walking into the café, Mark's doctor was walking out carrying a take-out drink container.

"Ah, Mark's fiancée again."

Rose gave a small giggle. "Yes, it's me again."

"You'll be happy to know he might be coming home to you tomorrow. I'll be here around six in the morning doing my rounds, and if all's good he can go home."

"Thank you, Doctor. I'm so happy he'll be home soon."

He smiled and gave her a nod and kept walking. Rose found Tulip at the counter paying for the coffee and the soda.

Tulip saw Rose as she walked away from the counter. "What are you doing here?"

"We might as well sit down for a few minutes because Mark has visitors."

Tulip raised his take out coffee. "The coffee will get cold."

"It'll stay hot for ages in that container."

The two girls sat down at one of the tables. "Who's visiting him?"

"Three guesses."

"I'd reckon I would only need two. Becky and Lucy."

"That's right. We heard them coming and he asked me not to leave him alone with them for too long."

Tulip raised her eyebrows. "That's good. That means he doesn't like them and he likes you." Tulip sucked on her straw while still keeping her eyes fixed on Rose.

"Do you think so?"

"It's pretty obvious if you ask me."

Rose sighed. "I wish I knew for certain."

"Ask him."

Rose gasped. "I couldn't."

Tulip shrugged. "There are many instances in the Bible where women did bold things regarding men. It worked for them. Anyway, so much for our plan of me talking with them. It might work if we head back now."

"*Nee*, just stay here."

While Tulip continued encouraging Rose to be more forthright with Mark, Rose considered that maybe her sister could be right. In the past, Mark had revealed how he'd felt, so maybe the time had come for her to do the same. Especially now that she had competition. If she didn't do something now, it might be too late. She wasn't an expert on love. All she knew was that her days were much better and happier with Mark in them.

"We should go now and take him his coffee," Tulip said when she finished her soda.

"I hope they've gone by now." Rose stood and pushed her chair under the table.

"If they haven't, we will just give him his coffee and then leave. Or did you want to stay? It's up to you."

"I think we'll just give him the coffee and then go. It'll be too awkward to stay around there with them there."

"I agree."

When they got back to Mark's hospital room, the two girls had made themselves comfortable. They looked like they'd be there until the visiting hours were over. After Tulip had handed Mark the coffee, Mark shot Rose a pleading look that said, 'save me.' Rose had to stifle a giggle. At that moment, she knew for certain that he liked her and no one else.

Chapter Twenty-Three

As for God, his way is perfect; the word of the Lord is tried: he is a buckler to all them that trust in him.

2 Samuel 22:31

The next day, Rose entered the hospital alone and hurried to room 209. Today was the day that the doctor had said Mark might be released.

Rose poked her head around the doorway of Mark's room and saw him sitting up in bed looking brighter.

"There you are," Mark said.

She walked to his bedside and then sat close to him on the bed. "*Jah*, here I am."

"You don't have to come here every day, Rosie."

"Of course I do. Tulip's looking after the stall today and everything's just fine. Are you getting out today?"

"Before I answer that, do you have any idea where my fiancée is?"

Rose frowned at him. "What do you mean?"

"My doctor keeps talking to me about my fiancée. Tell your fiancée this, tell her that, this is something your fiancée needs to know. I'm just wondering where she is, that's all." He dipped his head when Rose giggled. "Have you seen her?"

"I told him we were engaged the first day you were here. I've run into him two more times and he thinks I'm your fiancée."

"Oh, it's you?"

Rose nodded. She figured she'd made him wait long enough. He'd always been honest and held nothing back. She took hold of his hand. "Mark, do you still want to marry me like you used to?"

"I've always wanted to marry you, Rosie, always. That's something that'll never change as long as the sun keeps coming up every morning and sets every evening."

Peace swept over Rose and she knew in her heart that this man would never fail her or let her down in any way. She didn't want to go on without him in her life. It had taken her some time, and certainly more time than her parents were happy about, to find the perfect man for her. "Will you marry me, Mark?"

He smiled and stared at her for some time before he spoke. "Are you serious right now, Rosie? Don't joke with me about something like this."

"I've never been more serious." She leaned forward and placed her lips softly on his knowing she was kissing her husband—the one who had been made just for her. She pulled back.

"We're getting married, then, it seems."

Rose smiled at him and all was right with her world. "I'm glad."

"As soon as we possibly can?" he asked.

"*Jah*, very soon."

"That's all I've ever wanted, Rosie. That's all. I don't know why it took you so long to see that I was the man for you."

"It probably shouldn't have taken me so long, but it did."

"None of that matters now that we're together. This is the happiest day of my life."

When she saw him blinking back tears, she laughed and fought back tears of her own. "Don't you cry, or I'll cry and I won't be able to stop."

"Cry? I never cry. Well, maybe just a little every time someone accepts my marriage proposal."

Rose laughed. "Exactly how many marriage proposals have you given out?"

"Only ever the one. And I was right. I knew if I waited for you long enough you'd marry me." He squeezed her hand.

Rose held his hand tightly while she thought back to over a year ago. He'd always said there was never anybody else for him. It didn't matter now that he wasn't tall and handsome. He was Mark, and that was all she needed. Contentment and peace flooded her heart.

Three months later...

Mrs. Nancy Yoder leaned against the wall of her house. This was the first wedding that had taken place at her home. She looked over at Mark and Rose as they talked to one another at their wedding table in the yard. Her oldest daughter was finally married, and if it hadn't been for her pushing Rose, it might never have happened.

Mark had been an excellent choice of a husband for her daughter. She wondered why she hadn't seen sooner how Mark was the one.

Nancy sighed. She was tired. She had just, with the help of five other women, served over three hundred people for the wedding breakfast.

It had been an exhausting eighteen months trying to get

Rose married off. Firstly encouraging her, goading her, giving her ultimatums, and then leaving her alone. Now, her oldest daughter was finally married and she'd found someone who didn't mind that she was so tall and gangly.

Her sons, Peter and Trevor were married, along with Rose, so that left only Tulip, and then the twins, Daisy and Lily. She was halfway there; three children were married and three were left. With Tulip about to turn twenty, there was no time to waste. She looked around amongst the food tables set up in the yard, searching for Tulip. She finally saw her at the far end of the yard talking with three young men who appeared very interested in what she had to say.

"Ah, that looks like a fine start. I'll wander over there and find out who they are." She was pretty certain one was from their community, and the other two were visiting. In her ideal world, her daughters wouldn't go far from home when they married. If she managed things just so, she would see to it that what she wanted came to pass.

When she heard a squeal and raucous laughter, she looked and saw the twins playing with children. Nancy shook her head. A trip to the bishop might be required for those two. Out of her four daughters, Tulip was her smart one, Rose was the soft and gentle one, and the twins—the twins seemed to be a lost cause. As Nancy walked over to Tulip, to find out more about the young men she was speaking with, Nancy shook her head about the twins—they were a puzzle for later.

* * * * *

Chapter One

Harmony Creek Hollow, New York

The day had started out as Jeremiah Stoltzfus had planned.

It didn't stay that way after a woman dropped into his arms.

For most men, playing the hero for a beautiful woman would have been a dream come true. But most men didn't discover that woman trespassing on a tumble-down farm in northern New York. A farm Jeremiah couldn't wait to call his own.

He'd been invited by the current owner to visit when he reached Harmony Creek. In a couple of days the farm would be his.

At dawn Jeremiah had left his family's home in Paradise Springs, Pennsylvania. He was joining others to build a new Amish settlement near the Vermont border. He'd made arrangements during the past few months, purchasing the farm based on a few photographs sent by his Realtor. After saying goodbye to his *mamm*, brothers and sisters along with their spouses and *kinder* and knowing it was unlikely he'd see them again for a year, he'd taken a train north to Albany. There, he was met by a van, which drove him the last fifty miles to Harmony Creek Hollow.

The valley edging the creek was set outside the tiny town of Salem. Rolling hills covered with trees and meadows would support dairy farms for the Amish families moving into the area.

The owner of the sixty-acre farm he was buying, Rudy Bamberger, had invited him to stop by before the closing in two days. Jeremiah suspected the old man wanted to size him up first.

Rudy had already asked him a lot of questions through Kitty Vasic, Jeremiah's Realtor. Personal questions that Kitty told Jeremiah he didn't have to answer. However, Jeremiah had no problem with the questions because the old man had been selling his family's farm. Jeremiah had written a long letter, explaining his background and his plans for the farm and his future. His answers must have satisfied Rudy because the old man accepted his offer on the farm the next day.

When he'd arrived, Jeremiah had carried his two bags as he crossed the snowy yard past neglected barns. No tracks had been visible. Nothing had gone in or out of the big barn since the last snowstorm. Allowing himself a quick glance at the other outbuildings, which needed, as he'd known, a lot of repairs, he'd walked through the freshly fallen snow to the main house.

The large rambling home had a porch running along the front and the side facing the barn. Through a stand of spruce trees, he could see another house, where a tenant family once would have lived. The few remaining shutters hung awkwardly at the windows, a sure sign the house was a fixer-upper too.

He looked forward to beginning—and finishing—the

tasks ahead of him as he made the farm viable again. His skills as a woodworker would be useful while renovating the barns and the sap house near the sugar bush farther up the hill.

He'd climbed onto the porch and set down his bags before he knocked snow off his well-worn work boots. He'd gone directly to the side door. Rudy had told him to use that door when he arrived.

"Don't knock," the most recent letter had instructed him. "My ears don't work like they used to, and I don't want you standing in the cold while you bang and bang. Come in and give a shout."

He'd thrown the door open. "Rudy, are you here?"

A shriek had come from close to the ceiling. He'd looked up to see a ladder wobbling. A dark-haired woman stood at the very top, her arms windmilling.

He leaped into the small room as she fell. After years of being tossed shocks of corn and hay bales, he caught her easily. He jumped out of the way, holding her to him as the ladder crashed to the linoleum floor. His black wool hat tumbled off his head and rolled toward the wall.

"Oh, my!" gasped the woman.

She was, he noted because her face was close to his, very pretty. Her pleated *kapp* was flat unlike the heart-shaped ones his sisters wore. Beneath it, her hair was so black it gleamed with bluish fire in the fading sunlight coming through the door and tall windows. Her brown eyes were large with shock in her warmly tanned face where a few freckles emphasized her high cheekbones. She wore a pale pink dress with white and green flowers scattered across it in a subtle pattern. No Amish woman from Paradise Springs would use such fabric. It must be allowed in the new settlement along Harmony Creek. What else would be different here?

But first things first.

"Are you okay?" he asked, not surprised she wasn't the only one who sounded breathless. His heart had slammed against his chest when he saw her teetering. And from the moment he'd looked into her lustrous eyes, taking a deep breath had seemed impossible.

"I'm fine. I had just a little farther to go. Just a little…" Her voice trailed away as the shuddering ladder, which had landed on its side, clattered to the floor.

Jeremiah frowned. There was nothing on the wall to prevent her from falling. He saw that the ruined wallpaper and chipped crown molding along with scraps of paper she'd already pulled off were piled on the floor. Why was she tearing off wallpaper in Rudy's house?

"Who are you?" he asked at the same time she did.

"I'm Jeremiah Stoltzfus," he answered. "You are…?"

"Mercy Bamberger." Her face shifted into a polite smile, and he guessed she'd collected her wits that had been scattered by fear. "Thanks for catching me."

"Why are you here?"

Instead of answering, she said, "You can put me down."

Jeremiah was astonished his curiosity about why she was in what would be his house had let him forget—for a second—that he was still cradling her in his arms. He set her on her feet, but caught her by the elbow when she trembled like a slim branch in a thunderstorm.

Hearing uneven thumps upstairs and hoping they heralded Rudy's arrival, he steered her to the left. There, a staircase was half-hidden behind a partially closed door. Seating her on the bottom step, he picked up his hat as he asked, "Are you all right?"

"I am."

He didn't believe her, because her skin had a gray tint

and her voice quivered. He wouldn't push her because
he guessed she was embarrassed by the circumstances.
But one question remained: What was Mercy Bamberger
doing in his house?

"Bamberger?" he asked aloud. "Like Rudy Bamberger?"

"Yes. Do you know my grandfather?"

Well, that explained who she was and why she was
in the house. Glancing up the stairs, his eyes widened
when he saw a shadow slip across the top. It was far too
small for a grown man and appeared to have four legs.

He watched, saying nothing as he realized the silhouette belonged to a *kind*. A little girl, who looked about
seven years old, had braided hair as black as Mercy's.
She leaned on metal crutches with cuffs to go around
her skinny arms. Her legs were encased in plastic and
Velcro from the tops of her black sneakers to her knobby
knees. Who was she?

As if he'd asked the question aloud, the little girl
cried, "Mommy!" Rushing at a pace that forced his heart
into his throat again, because he feared she'd fall, the
kind flung her arms around Mercy's neck. "Are you
okay?"

"I'm fine," Mercy reassured her.

The *kind* glanced at him with a scowl. "I heard the
ladder fall and—"

"I'm fine, Sunni." She hugged the little girl. "Jeremiah kept me from getting hurt."

"Who?"

"Jeremiah." Mercy pushed herself to her feet and
swung the little girl off the steps. She kept herself between the *kind* and him, showing she didn't trust him,
though he'd saved her from a broken bone or worse.
"He's Jeremiah." Without looking at him, she added,
"Jeremiah, this is my daughter, Sunni."

Again he fought not to ask the questions battering at his lips. The *kind* was unquestionably Asian, and her eyes, like Mercy's, glistened like dark brown mud in a sun-washed puddle. She also wore plain clothing with a small print.

Comprehension struck him. Mercy and her daughter weren't Amish. They dressed like the Mennonite women who lived near Paradise Springs. He searched his mind, but couldn't recall if his Realtor had mentioned anything about Rudy living plain. He glanced up at the electric light hanging from the ceiling. Some plain folks used electricity.

Too many questions needed answers.

Right away.

"Hi, Sunni," he said, because he didn't want to upset the little girl or her *mamm* more.

She aimed another frown at him before turning her back on him. When she didn't answer him, Mercy asked the *kind* why she'd been upstairs. He thought she was dismayed the little girl had gone on the stairs by herself until Mercy said, "Be extra careful. Don't forget the floors aren't safe."

"I stayed away from those, Mommy." Sunni raised her left crutch and tapped the floor beside her. "I do that to check before I go in." Without a pause, she asked, "Can I have a cookie?"

"One," Mercy said with a smile. "Put the bag clip on after you get your cookie."

"Okaaaay," Sunni replied in the same tone Jeremiah had used as a *kind* when his own *mamm* said something he deemed obvious.

He smiled, but again the little girl acted as if he were invisible before she drew her arms from the cuffs on the crutches. Leaning them against the wall, she hurried through a doorway to the right. He guessed it must lead to the kitchen.

His grin vanished as he glanced around the room. Rudy called it his everything room. Hooks on the wall showed where coats, hats and bonnets could be hung. The bare floor was scraped from years of barn boots on it, and the tattered wallpaper was a grubby white. It might once have been a brighter color. The room was furnished with a rickety table and a battered sofa covered with a worn blanket. A desk had a book under one leg to keep it steady on the sloping floor. The interior of the house was in worse condition than the outside. The photographs sent by the Realtor had been misleading.

Had he failed to examine them closely enough in his eagerness to buy the farm and get started on making his dream come true? No, he'd peered at each picture through a magnifying glass to discover every detail. He knew the kitchen cabinets were painted dull brown, and there was electricity in the house. He planned to remove the latter as soon as the papers were signed.

Jeremiah picked up the ladder and raised it against the wall again. Checking it was solidly in place, he looked at Mercy. He was curious why she was peeling paper off the wall in what would be his house. He could understand if she wanted to take one of the pictures of the farm hanging on a fake brick wall behind the desk, because the farm was her *grossdawdi*'s. In the silence, the *tick-tock* of a wall clock in the kitchen was loud.

Jeremiah appraised the room again. He intended to use it for the farm's office, as he guessed Rudy had. It was one plan among the many he had. His brothers teased him about having to have every detail set in place before he acted, but trying to find knots in a piece of wood before he began working on it had kept him from wasting time when building a piece of furniture. Being as cautious in his other endeavors seemed wise.

Though he knew, too well, the best of plans could fall apart. He'd thought his future was set with Emmarita Kramer, but she'd jumped the fence and married an *Englisch* guy she'd met at an auction Jeremiah had taken her to. She'd never broken the courtship off with Jeremiah, just left. He should forgive her and forget his shock, but when he hadn't been able to do either, he'd decided on a clean start in the new Harmony Creek settlement.

Hearing a throat cleared and knowing Mercy was trying to get his attention, he turned. She was shorter than he'd realized. The top of her head barely reached his shoulder. As she stuck several vagrant strands of black hair beneath her pleated *kapp*, she regarded him coolly. She was, he could tell from the set of her taut lips, as curious about him as her daughter had been.

He had a lot of things he wanted to ask her too, but he waited for her to speak first.

She took one step, then another toward him, though she was at a disadvantage because she had to tilt her head to meet his eyes. Then, seeing the determination in them, he wondered if she saw her height as a liability or a way to surprise those who underestimated her.

"You never answered my question," she said.

"Which one?" He couldn't remember what she'd asked him, and he refused to be put on the defensive in what would be his own home.

"The important one. What are you doing here?"

"I came to see Rudy Bamberger." He frowned. "You said he's your *grossdawdi*."

She nodded.

"Then I'm surprised he didn't tell you I'd be coming here today."

"Why?"

He didn't think she was being cagey on purpose. Until now, she'd been straightforward. "He invited me to come and look around."

She shook her head. "I don't understand why."

"Didn't he tell you he's selling me his farm?"

Mercy Bamberger was shocked speechless. Had she hit her head when she'd dropped into Jeremiah Stoltzfus's strong arms after trying to grab another strip of wallpaper? She'd made a mess of this conversation from the get-go.

With the ancient Adirondacks to the west and the gentle Green Mountains to the east, the farm had been a haven for her from the first time she'd come to visit the man she called Grandpa Rudy. It offered the very thing she'd lost and didn't think she'd ever find again. Home. How desperate she'd been for a sanctuary! And how precious it seemed as the promise she'd held within her heart for the past decade was being fulfilled.

She couldn't mess it up. Already she'd made the mistake of not keeping a closer eye on Sunni. Her daughter had been born with a congenital curiosity not diminished by her physical challenges. Mercy's determination that the little girl should do anything a regular kid could allowed Sunni to indulge her quick and inquiring mind. Telling Sunni not to investigate the rooms upstairs because the floors were unsafe must have convinced her to find out how dangerous they were.

Mercy was letting herself get distracted by a handsome stranger who appeared to be a few years older than her twenty-five years. His bright blue eyes that had been shadowed by his black wool hat identified him as one of the Amish farmers moving into the hollow. Grandpa

Rudy had told her about the new settlement in one of his letters. He'd been writing to her every week since she was eleven years old, the year she'd been adopted by his son and daughter-in-law and given a chance to have a new life and the loving family she'd feared she'd never have again.

She was startled how far up she had to look to meet Jeremiah's eyes. Few Amish men she'd met had been as tall as he was. If his ruddy hair hadn't been cut in the plain style and he wasn't wearing a simple light blue shirt along with black suspenders and broad-fall trousers beneath his black coat, she wouldn't have guessed this very good-looking man was Amish.

Scolding herself, she recalled how Graham Rapp was easy on the eyes too, but he'd broken her heart by showing how much a "mama's boy" he was by choosing his mother when Mercy refused to be second. She must not let herself be beguiled by an attractive man again. Not when so much was on the line with her plans for the farm and the changes it could make in many young lives.

But the Amish were well-known for their honesty. So why was Jeremiah talking nonsense about Grandpa Rudy selling him the farm?

"I think you're mistaken," she said, hoping her voice didn't quake with the strong emotions rushing through her like lightning in a summer sky. "My grandfather didn't mention anything about selling Come Along Farm."

"Come Along Farm?"

"That's the name he gave the farm when I was little. He urged us to come along and keep up with him while he did chores, so we called it Come Along Farm."

"He didn't tell you he's selling me the farm?"

"No!"

"I'm sorry to take you by surprise," he said gently, "but I'll be closing the day after tomorrow."

"Impossible!" Her voice squeaked, and she took a steadying breath. Sounding as young as Sunni wouldn't help. And she didn't want her raised voice to bring her daughter from the kitchen to investigate. The little girl was upset enough already to have to leave their Mennonite community and Mercy's parents in central New York, and Mercy hadn't missed the glares Sunni had shot at Jeremiah. When she and Graham ended their ill-advised engagement, her daughter had been caught up in the aftermath and no longer trusted men she didn't know. Mercy's attempts to reassure Sunni that the little girl had nothing to do with the breakup hadn't helped.

"It's not impossible. I've got the paperwork in my suitcase on the porch. If you want to see it—"

"I don't have interest in seeing what can't be legitimate. It sounds as if someone has played a horrible prank on you, Jeremiah. I'm sorry." She was, because she guessed he'd traveled for hours or days to get there. "But the farm's not for sale."

He opened his mouth to protest, then closed it. Taking a deep breath, he released it. In a calm tone she doubted she could emulate, he said, "There's no sense in arguing. Why don't you get your *grossdawdi*, and we'll settle this?"

"I can't."

"Why not?"

She blinked on sudden tears. "Because he's dead."

When Jeremiah's face became ashen, Mercy wondered if she should tell him to take a seat. It must have been seconds, but it felt like a year before he asked, "Rudy is dead?"

"Yes." She swallowed hard past the lump in her throat.

"When?"

"Last week. It was a massive heart attack. He was buried the day before yesterday." As she spoke, she found it impossible to believe the vital, vigorous man was gone.

Rudy Bamberger had been more than a grandfather to her. He'd been her best friend, the one who had welcomed her into the family after her life had hit bottom. Rudy hadn't been a replacement for Abuelita, her beloved grandmother, who had raised her when she was called Mercedes in a tiny apartment in the Bronx. Abuelita had died two weeks after Mercy's tenth birthday, and everything in Mercy's life had changed, including her name. Yet Grandpa Rudy had made her feel as if she belonged among the people who were so different from those she'd known in the city. His love had been unconditional, and she'd returned it.

"I'm sorry," Jeremiah said with sincerity.

She wished he'd been trite instead of genuine because one thing hadn't changed. He wanted to take away the farm that was her final gift from Grandpa Rudy. How often she'd sat on the old man's lap and talked about taking care of the apple orchard or making maple syrup as he did each spring or what color she would paint the big bedroom! He'd humored her, even when her paint choices went from pink to purple to red and black over the years.

But Jeremiah was saying her grandfather had intended to sell the farm to him.

"But Grandpa Rudy told me the farm would be mine after he passed away."

"Then why would he sign a purchase agreement with me?"

Mercy shook herself from her mental paralysis. She

hated admitting she couldn't guess why her grandfather would break his promise to her.

"Mommy, what's wrong?"

Shocked she hadn't noticed Sunni in the kitchen doorway, Mercy put her arm around her daughter's narrow shoulders. "Nothing that can't be fixed," she replied with a smile.

Over the child's head, she shot Jeremiah a frown, warning him not to upset Sunni. She didn't want her daughter to feel as if her world was being taken away from her—again—as it must have when Sunni traveled from Korea to what was supposed to be her forever home. It hadn't been, because her adoptive parents, who'd changed her name from Kim Sun-Hee to Sunni, couldn't handle having a daughter who wore leg braces. Sunni had been returned to Social Services as if she were a set of curtains that didn't match the furniture. A disrupted adoption was the name given to it. Or a failed placement. The latter fit better, because it sure felt like a failure for the child involved.

As Mercy had learned herself fifteen years ago when she'd been the one given away by what she'd thought would be her forever family. If the Bambergers hadn't been there to take her in… No, she didn't want to think of that awful time.

Again, she warned herself to focus on the present, not the past. And her and Sunni's future. She had to stop letting her emotions take over. She needed to be logical. Building Come Along Farm into a retreat for city kids would require her to face a lot of bureaucracy on local and state levels. She must be ready to stand up for what she wanted.

"Sunni, if you go and get the book we were reading, I'll meet you in the living room once I'm finished here."

The little girl looked from her to Jeremiah, then nodded. "Okay, Mommy."

Mercy said nothing as Jeremiah watched Sunni hobble away. There was no pity in his expression, and she was grateful. Too many people felt sorry for Sunni, calling her a "poor little thing." Sunni was one of the strongest people Mercy knew and had learned to walk through perseverance and hard work. If only Mercy could help her heal from the emotional wounds she'd suffered, but those would take more time.

As soon as the little girl was out of earshot, Mercy said, "I guess I should see the purchase agreement you say my grandfather signed."

Jeremiah hooked a thumb toward the door. "Give me a minute, and I'll dig out the paperwork I've got."

She considered locking the door, but that wouldn't solve the problem. Instead, she held the door open while he brought in two scuffed duffel bags.

Closing the door, she said nothing while he opened one bag and found a manila envelope. He withdrew a sheaf of pages and sorted through them. In the middle of the stack, he pulled out several and offered them to her.

"Here's everything I got from your *grossdawdi* through my Realtor," he said without a hint of emotion.

Mercy didn't look to discover if compassion had slipped into his gaze. This time for her. She wanted it no more than Sunni would have. When he handed her the pages, his work-roughened skin brushed against her fingers. Sensation arced between them like electricity, and she jerked her hand away. Being attracted to the man who insisted he was buying her family's farm would be stupid.

If he had the same reaction, she couldn't tell because

she carefully kept her gaze on the papers. She scanned each page, her heart sinking lower and lower. Everything looked aboveboard, and she recognized her grandfather's scrawled signature on the bottom of each page. She didn't stop to decipher every bit of legalese, but grasped enough to know Grandpa Rudy was selling the farm to Jeremiah Stoltzfus.

Just as Jeremiah claimed.

"But my grandfather died," she whispered. "Doesn't that change things?"

"I don't know. This is the first time I've ever bought property." He gave her a lopsided grin that lifted her traitorous heart once more.

Paying it no attention, she returned the papers to him and he put them in his bag. No one could answer the question gnawing at her most. Why would her grandfather promise her the property and then decide to sell it without telling her? She'd often mentioned her plans for the farm. Hadn't he read her letters? Yes, he had, because he'd responded to things in them. But never, she realized with a jolt of dismay, had he written anything about her intention to make Come Along Farm a sanctuary for city youngsters like the one she'd enjoyed when she was a Fresh Air kid years ago, escaping for two amazing weeks each summer from the steam bath of the Bronx.

"I'm not sure what we should do," he said when she remained silent.

"Me either." For the first time she looked straight into his brilliantly blue eyes. He must realize what she was about to say she meant with all her heart. "However, you need to know I'm not going to relinquish my family's farm to you or anyone else."

"But—"

"We moved in a couple of days ago. We're not giving it up." She crossed her arms over her chest. "It's our *home*."

Chapter Two

Jeremiah had to select his words with care. He didn't know if he'd be allowed to close on the farm as scheduled. He'd never heard of a person dying before property was transferred, because in Paradise Springs most farms were handed down from one generation to the next.

As Mercy said Rudy had meant to do with this farm. He'd changed his mind, but why?

Until he spoke with Kitty Vasic, his Realtor, and got her advice, he didn't know what the outcome of this sticky situation would be. Mercy wasn't going to back down. That much was clear. If their situations were reversed, he suspected he'd be as unwilling to compromise. He *was* unwilling to compromise.

There wasn't room to. Either the farm was going to be his…or it wasn't.

"It's late," he said when he realized Mercy was waiting for him to say something. "I doubt Kitty's office is open. Do you know anyone nearby who has a phone I could use?"

As if in answer to him, a faint ringing came from beyond the living room. He glanced at Mercy and saw she was as surprised as he was at the unexpected sound.

"Phone!" called Sunni. "I'll get it."

"No! I'll get it." Mercy spun on her heel and ran toward the sound.

Jeremiah followed, too curious to wait. He paid no attention to the large living room as he went after Mercy through what looked like a storage room and then into a bedroom. It was draped in shadows, but a single greenish light glared off to one side.

Mercy grabbed the cordless phone and jabbed at a button. Holding it to her ear, she asked, "Hello?"

The faint buzz of a voice reached him, but he couldn't discern words. His eyes widened when she held the phone out to him.

"It's for you," she said.

"For me?"

"Yes, unless you know another Jeremiah Stoltzfus."

He knew three others in Paradise Springs alone. Taking the phone, he said, "This is Jeremiah Stoltzfus."

"Hi, Jeremiah," replied a strained female voice. "This is Kitty Vasic. I know Rudy invited you to the farm, so I thought I'd catch you there. We need to talk. Rudy Bamberger is dead."

"*Ja*, I know." He glanced toward Mercy, but she'd gone to stand by a window. Talking about this was uncomfortable. For him, the farm and his future were at stake, but she'd lost her *grossdawdi*. He didn't like the idea of losing his opportunity to buy this farm, but he also disliked the idea of taking Mercy's home.

"I've got something tonight I can't get out of," Kitty said. "How about I come over tomorrow afternoon?"

"Tomorrow afternoon should be fine." What else could he say?

"Good. I'll meet you at the farm around one."

He thanked her. Tilting the phone toward the faint

light coming through the window, he found the button to end the call. He set it in its holder. It chirped once, and then its glow faded.

"That was my Realtor," Jeremiah said. "She's coming over tomorrow afternoon around one to discuss what happens next."

A soft *click* sounded in the room before a lamp came on by the side of a bed with a headboard taller than he was. It was carved with a great tree filled with birds and other beasts gathered below it. He realized the lamp must have been connected to a timer.

"I can make myself scarce," Mercy replied.

He shook his head. "Don't. You should be here so you can ask Kitty your questions. In fact, you should contact the Realtor your *grossdawdi* used and have him here."

"I have no idea who that is."

"His name is on the paperwork I signed. Why don't I get it? It might have his phone number. You can call him and get him here too."

She rubbed her hands together. "Thank you, Jeremiah. You're being nice about this."

"Me? You didn't throw me out on my ear when I barged in."

When she smiled, it was as if another dozen lights had turned on. "I couldn't throw you out after you saved me from my own foolishness."

The pleasant warmth buzzed through him again as his gaze connected with hers. He looked away. Until he knew what was going to happen with the farm, he needed to keep his distance.

Turning on his heel, he went to where he'd left his bags. He'd get the information she needed and then…

And then what?

Tell her he'd planned to stay here tonight? He couldn't

insist Mercy and her little girl find another place tonight. He wasn't sure what, under the circumstances, would happen if he left the property before the disposition of the farm was decided. Possession being nine-tenths of the law…or something like that.

Don't miss
AN AMISH ARRANGEMENT by Jo Ann Brown,
available January 2018 wherever
Love Inspired® books and ebooks are sold.

www.Harlequin.com